CHRISTMAS ON ICE

CYPRESSVILLE SMALL TOWN ROMANCE

KRISTEN TASSIN

TASTEC INK

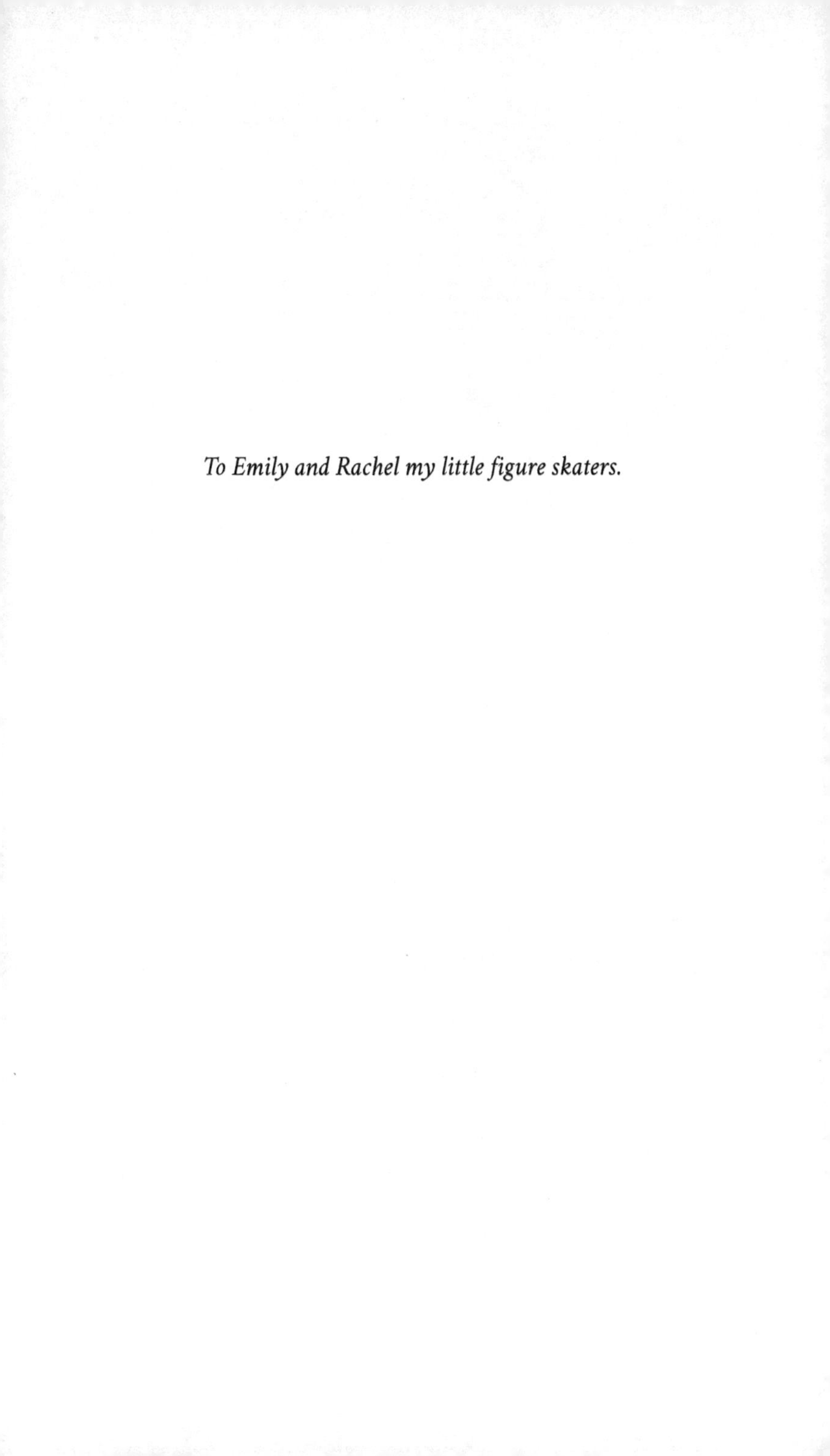

To Emily and Rachel my little figure skaters.

Copyright © 2nd Edition 2024, 1st Edition 2021 by Kristen Tassin

All rights reserved.

No part of this book may be reproduced in any form or by any electronic or mechanical means, including information storage and retrieval systems, without written permission from the author, except for the use of brief quotations in a book review.

All characters, locales, institutions, religions, myths, and events are entirely fictitious. Any similarity to real persons, living or dead, is coincidental and not intended by the author.

Proofreader- Heather F. Theriot

Cover Design- KTK Design

CHRISTMAS ON ICE

CHAPTER ONE

SKATING ON THIN ICE

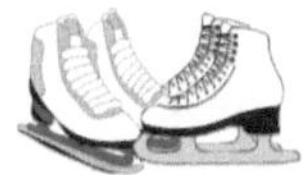

"One more time," Coach LaBoulay shouted across the ice. Sarah blew out a breath and skated in a circle with her hands braced on her hips. She had been practicing quads for her routine for the past two hours. She perfected the quadruple toe loop and quadruple Salchow and could do the triple axle and lutz, but to make it to the championships, Sarah needed to up her game and perform quads. Coach wanted her to aim for six in a row. At twenty-two, she was past the typical prime for most women's figure skating competitors, trying to make it to the Olympics for the first time.

Sarah finally had her chance. When she was sixteen, Sarah nearly lost her dedication to getting back on the ice after she fractured her ankle at practice right before the World Championships until her grandpa told her one of his many phrases to keep her going: *"Life is like a gumbo. Sometimes, when the roux burns, you have to start from scratch, add all the ingredients, and it only gets better the longer it simmers."*

"Sarah!" Coach LaBoulay shouted her name again.

"Alright, already," she shouted, skating around the rink.

She got into position, feeling the wind of her speed pass across her face, the exhilaration in her muscles prepping for the spin. She was in the air, mentally counting her rotations. "One, two, three, four, five," she heard her teammates start to clap prematurely, breaking her concentration. Her momentum failed, and she landed shakily, twisting her ankle slightly, but she shook it off.

Coach LaBoulay shouted, "Again!"

Sarah skated the rink twice, doing a few forward and backward moves and a small jump to test her ankle. It felt fine, so she went for it, this time tuning everything out around her.

"I can do this," she breathed, picked up her momentum, and was once more spinning in the air, counting the rotations in her head. "One, two, three, four, five, six."

She did it!

Excitement coursed through her veins, and a huge smile graced her lips as she tuned into everyone cheering—or that was the case until she landed hard on the sore ankle. The loud pop and the instant pain that radiated up her leg dropped her to the ice, landing hard and sliding a bit. She lay in pain, staring up at the ceiling of the rink, tears streaming down her face.

Coach skated over to her side and leaned over her. "You alright?" He knelt beside Sarah when she shook her head.

Sarah couldn't stop the tears from flooding her eyes. Her voice trembled. "I think it's broken."

Coach LaBoulay sighed, "Let me see." He straightened her leg, unlaced the boot, and started taking it off. Sarah involuntarily moaned out in pain. She bit her lips together and tried not to show how badly it hurt.

"Mariah," the coach called out to one of the younger teammates. "Go get the wheelchair. "Jessamine, let the medic know that we will need X-rays." The girls took off.

"Let the ice keep the ankle cool until I get you in the back."

Coach stood up and skated off the ice to the other girls and started having them do skills practice on the other end of the rink.

Sarah knew her career was over. Her grampa's words, which had given her confidence only a few minutes earlier, didn't comfort her anymore. She was too old now to start over. Why did she push herself for six quads for the World Championships? She should have saved that for the Olympics once she was ready. That dream would never happen; it was now null and void.

Two months flew by, and Sarah's grampa left to return to Cypressville, LA, her hometown. He needed to return to his farm. He had left it in the care of friends long enough, and with the Thanksgiving holiday approaching, they needed to spend it with their family. Sarah still had the boot on and couldn't put more than twenty pounds on her ankle after surgery, but at least she could get around on crutches now.

Sarah's door opened, and in came her best friend, Jane. "Knock, knock," she said, rolling her suitcase behind her. I just saw Grampa George leave. He got in the cab that just delivered me. I'm so glad I got to see him. It's been so long."

Jane took a deep breath and was about to start talking again. But before she did, Sarah hurriedly interjected. "Thanks for coming up to spend Thanksgiving with me. I hate that I can't go home yet, but my therapy and medical expenses are all paid for here. I didn't want to put Grampa out more than I already have."

"Girl, you need to stop that. Your grampa would give you

the stars and the moon if you asked, and before you interject with your grumbling," Jane got her there because Sarah was about to say something. "Your grampa doesn't care what you do as long as you're happy. He told me he prayed for a Christmas miracle for you this year. He doesn't like seeing you so sad."

Sarah sighed. "I know. He told me the same thing, but my life's dream is gone. There is nothing left for me to do now."

Jane rolled her eyes. "Good grief, Sarah, you are acting as if the world has ended. You are only twenty-two, and you've never dated. Maybe it's time you find yourself a man to focus on instead of only the ice." Then Jane chuckled to herself.

"What's so funny about me finding a guy?" Sarah asked, a bit peeved that her friend thought her dating was laughable.

Jane blushed, "It's stupid, but I just thought, I hope you find Mr. Nice instead of Mr. Ice."

Sarah groaned. "Geez, Jane, your jokes have not improved over the years." She hobbled to the sofa and sat down, leaning her crutches next to her. "How long can you stay? Please tell me you can stay at least a week?"

Jane followed Sarah, sat on the other end of the sofa, and leaned back on the cushion. "I'm exhausted. That flight was not the best." She peeked open one eye and glanced at Sarah. "I can stay until Sunday to spend Thanksgiving with you and black Friday. It's been so long since we've been able to shop like crazy ladies. I hope you will be up for it. Do you still have the wheelchair? I don't mind pushing you everywhere so you don't get burnt out."

"Jane, how are you still breathing?" Sarah sometimes forgot how long-winded and fast-talking Jane could be.

Jane chuckled, "I had six cups of coffee at the airport during my layover. I wanted to make sure I didn't fall asleep and miss my connection, but now that I'm here, I want to crash."

Sarah stood back up and picked up her crutches. "Come along, then. Let me show you to our room so that you can get some sleep. Tomorrow, you get to go grocery shopping for Thanksgiving dinner while I go to physical therapy."

The following morning, Sarah woke up to the sun streaming on her face and the cold Autumn air freezing her room from the open window. "Jane," she shivered and pulled the covers to her chin. "Why are you hanging out the window like a fool when it's four degrees outside?"

Jane laughed, "It's not four degrees. It can't be more than forty."

Sarah sat up, "Celcius Jane, we're in Canada. It's not Fahrenheit."

Jane shut the window and turned around, facing Sarah. "I don't get it. You skate in an ice rink seven days a week. How can a little northerly wind make you all trembly cold."

"It's because I'm not moving around. Anyway, what were you doing?"

Jane breathed out a long sigh, "Enjoying the view; it's beautiful here. The leaves are red, orange, and yellow, and the wind is crisp and clean. To top it off, I can see the water from the window and smell freshly baked bread nearby. This area is so peaceful. Thank you so much for inviting me to stay with you. I am grateful now you talked me into getting my passport. I honestly never thought I would travel or fly in a plane anywhere. I thought I'd be stuck at home forever."

"Jane, we both need a life check. Like you told me, you are twenty-two and have a whole life ahead of you."

Jane shook her head. "I need to stop blabbering my mouth so much, then I won't have to hear my advice hit me in the face."

Sarah moved the covers back and shifted to hang her legs off the bed. She grabbed her crutches, leaning on the nightstand, and stood up. "Well, I better get ready. A cab will be here for me at nine to pick me up for my appointment."

"When you're done, there are fresh scones for breakfast," Jane said as Sarah headed to the bathroom.

"What time did you wake up?" Sarah asked, then yawned, still trying to wake up herself.

"Early. The smell from the bakery made me itch to make something, so I found my way to the store and bought a few baking goods. But I ran out of Canadian bills and need to go to the bank again later."

"You don't have to do that. I have provisional money for food; it's in the envelope next to the fridge, and you can take what you need out. I also have a list, but they may not have everything. You are a great cook, so I figured it would be incredible no matter what we have."

Jane made a noncommittal sound and said, "I forgot that they don't celebrate American Thanksgiving here, and I am an okay cook; nothing special."

"Yeah, right," Sarah said, walking out finally.

A few minutes later, the shower ended, and Jane sat at the kitchen island. Sarah picked up a scone, took a bite, and moaned as the scone melted in her mouth. "Yeah, right, you are only okay." She took another bite of her scone, "Seriously, this is heavenly. You could easily open your own bakery."

Jane shook her head. "No way that would mean I'd have to wake up at the crack of dawn to start baking, and I prefer to sleep in."

Sarah shook her head. "Um, weren't you the one up at the crack of dawn making scones this morning?"

"That is only because airline delays messed up my sleep. I will probably sleep in until after you get home from physical therapy every day. How is that going, by the way?"

Sarah closed her eyes and tilted her head back.

"That bad?" Jane asked.

"It's not bad; it's just why bother working so hard when I will never skate again. You know—my career is over, so I've been doing the bare minimum to get by so I can walk without these crutches."

"Hmm. I was wondering why you were taking longer to recover this time. When you had your first surgery, you worked your butt off to get back on the ice fast."

"There is no need to anymore. Coach LaBoulay called last night after you fell asleep and told me that he and the team were leaving at the end of the week. If I hadn't injured my ankle, I'd be flying to France now with my team and attending the competition. It was my last chance to get a gold medal to get into the Olympics, but nope, I'm not that lucky. I got the short end of the stick and broke my ankle and ruined my life." Sarah picked up her third scone. "So here I am, scarfing down scones because I don't have to keep my weight down anymore, I don't have to compete anymore, and I don't have a passion anymore; my life is over."

Jane rolled her eyes. "And I thought I was the dramatic one. Girl, I am telling you it's time to take your focus off of yourself, find one of the gorgeous tall Canadian men, and have fun for once. You've always been too focused. Why not be a typically young adult and have a fling, fall in love, and who knows, maybe you might even decide to get married and have a bunch of kids and make your own?" Jane looked up in thought and giggled.

"What now, you think it's comical that I could have kids?"

She chuckled again. "No, I was just imagining you having six kids, and they all tell you that they love the ice but want to be hockey players."

Sarah groaned. "Not in my house! I won't have any brutes in my little family. They will all be graceful figure skaters or something else altogether. I may never tell my children I was a pro skater."

A horn honked.

"That's my ride. I'll be back in about three hours." She got up and hobbled on her crutches. "Thanks again for going shopping for me. I have no clue what I will do when I'm on my own again."

"I don't mind, but you know Sarah, you can always come home. We have physical therapy places in Louisiana, too, you know."

Sarah sighed, "I know." She walked down the steps slowly and got into the cab. She did know, but she also knew that her dream would really be over once she went home. Going home meant she'd have to figure out a new life plan, and she wasn't quite ready for that reality.

CHAPTER TWO

I'M NOT THE PUCK

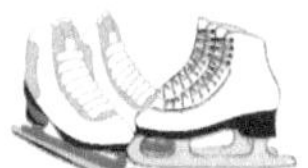

The air hung heavy with sweat and the satisfying scent of victory. Towels littered the floor, and the sounds of showers mingled with the post-game chatter. The Halifax Hurricanes won again, and Alex, the veteran center, stretched out on a bench, drying off his shaggy hair. A hard hand clapped his shoulder as Matthews, a veteran defenseman, sat beside him.

"Did you see the move Ivanov pulled in the third? Pure magic!"

Zelepi, the goalie, was heading to the shower and whipped his towel at Alex. "Better watch your back, Holstead, or you might lose your position as team idol."

Everyone laughed, and Alex threw a playful punch at Zelepi's arm.

Alex puffed out his chest and whipped his hair back, imitating a fashionista. "Hey, I still got a few good years left in me. I won't lose my mantle that easily, but I gotta admit a couple of these rookies might take me out in the next year or two, the way they are performing. I'm impressed."

Benson, Alex's best friend and the team's winger, joined in, "Are you talking about Ivanov?"

Alex nodded. Benson, a huge red-headed beast of a man with half his teeth missing, stuck his veneers in and then said, "That kid is fast as a bullet on the ice. Reminds me of myself at his age… only missing one thing."

"And that is?" Alex chuckled. Benson shook out his thick, curly red locks, splattering water droplets on them all. "These luxurious locks," he said, grinned, and "a new set of pearly whites."

Matthews grinned, "Speaking of hair, did you see the new defensemen, Jenö?" He whistled and shook his hand like he burned his fingers. He looked like he walked straight out of a boy band, so fragile."

Alex shook his head in humor. "Hey, don't judge a book by its cover, Matthews. Remember what happened last year with that "tough guy" rookie you went on about in the beginning? He was all bark and no bite, gotta give the newbie a chance to show us what he's got."

Matthews scoffed, "Yeah, yeah."

Alex watched Benson scan the room. He was giving each of the new members a once over, and as they caught his eye, he nodded to them individually. Being the captain, Benson liked to show the rookies who the team Alpha was, and at six-six, the tallest member of their time by two inches, Alex falling right behind him at six-four, the newbies showed him respect.

Benson turned to Matthews, "But seriously, even though some of these rookies look like babies, I like to believe they bring a fresh energy to the team. It keeps old dogs like us on our toes, right, Holstead?"

Alex nodded. "Absolutely. Competition breeds excellence. And who knows, maybe one of these kids will be the next big thing."

Zelepi emerged from the shower with his towel around his neck. "Just as long as they don't steal my starting spot, we all good." Louder, he shouted, "Rookies hear that? My crease, my rules!"

Everyone was laughing when the locker room door swung open. Coach Talbot was gruff and never smiled, but he was a well-respected coach in the NHL. He had just transferred to the Halifax Hurricanes two seasons before, and he, Alex, and Benson hit it off well. They tended to get drinks after a win, which was as loose as the two players ever saw their coach.

Coach Talbot whistled through his teeth. "Alright, alright, break it up. Celebrate tonight, but tomorrow, it's back to work. We got a long season ahead of us, especially you rookies," he shifted his fingers from his eyes to the five new guys. Tomorrow, we will start double the time on those drills."

The rookies, hanging back from the team's veterans, nodded eagerly. Alex watched them, a flicker of something akin to pride in his eyes. He had a good feeling about their team — change was coming.

Coach Talbot hung back and waited for everyone except Benson and Alex to leave.

"Holstead, I'm appointing you captain of the rookies for a couple of weeks. I want you to work one-on-one with Ivanov to get him up to speed with some of your signature moves. No drinks tonight because we have an early day, men."

Coach walked out, and Alex turned to Benson, "Long season indeed. And it seems it is full of surprises."

Benson whispered conspiratorially in Alex's ear. "One drink won't knock us down. We are two sturdy lads."

The men left the locker room rejuvenated from the win and ready to celebrate at the after-party Coach had no clue about.

The air thumped with music, and the post-game euphoria was tangible in the crowd at the bar downtown. Alex sat at the bar watching his teammates, with a woman on his side hanging on his every word and his best friend Benson on the other side kissing two different women on and off.

He wondered when they both became players with the women. The woman beside him ran a finger down his chest and whispered, "Let's go to my place for a private after-party."

Alex stood as if to leave, then remembered that he had to be ready for the morning's practice. He kissed her and looked at Benson. "Sorry, ladies. We have an early morning tomorrow."

Benson immediately dropped his arms from the girl's waist. "Way to ruin the party, man," but he looked to his companions with regret written all over it, "he's right. Maybe next time, though."

The ladies pouted and tried to convince Alex that they could still perform even with little sleep. Her words boosted Alex's drunken ego, and he almost changed his mind about heading home with the lady. Then he realized he didn't even know her name. When had he become so shallow? He turned, picked up the shot on the bar, and gulped it down.

Zelepi interrupted, "Ladies, there's no need for long faces; I'm free tonight." Like a flock of seagulls, the women latched on to Zelepi, leaving Benson and Alex.

Feeling his ego bruising after the woman left so quickly, Alex threw his arm around Benson, "You know, brother," he pointed to Ivanov, "he may be fast." He drank another shot, "I'll give him that."

Alex swayed a bit. The alcohol made his vision blur for a second. He caught himself on Benson. He held his hands on his shoulders and stared at him in his face, aiming for a whisper. He failed, and his voice rose instead. The words of the lady who left his side rang in his head that he was capable of doing anything these kids could do and, better, even drunk. His words slurred, "These punks haven't seen anything yet. Does the coach want me to show them the ropes tomorrow? It's more like I'll show them how a real champion plays!"

Benson, just as drunk, egged him on. "Give 'em hell tomorrow. I've got your back. Us veterans need to show these pipsqueaks who the real men are."

They both laughed. Zelepi, Matthews, and the ladies raised their glasses to them.

Slurring his words and suddenly feeling like a loser, Ivanov, his second, was fast as lightning and had a strong arm. He would be playing circles around Alex in a month with more training. Alex turned to Benson. "You know I still got it right. You saw me out there tonight. I made the win at the last second. I still have the golden touch."

Benson chuckled and squeezed Alex's shoulder, "Relax, Alex. Coach wouldn't have asked you specifically to train the rookie if you weren't the best. Just make sure you work them extra hard. Now let's get home, coach will be pissed if we don't have our heads on straight tomorrow."

Alex nodded, "Sounds good to me! This season's gonna be a piece of cake."

As they walked out, Alex lost his balance and fell into Benson.

Benson gave him a look of concern. "You can make it home?"

"Sure I can. You don't have to babysit me."

Benson had drank just as much as Alex had, but Benson

didn't seem nearly as phased. "You know what, I live closer. You can stay at my place tonight and head in to practice together. I will make you my hangover brew in the morning."

He got in the cab, leaned his head back, and fell asleep, completely forgetting what his best friend had said.

The four rookies were doing skate drills. The rhythmic scrape of blades echoing on the ice made Alex's head pound. Benson's hangover cure didn't work. His tongue was thick in his mouth, and his joints ached. His old knee injury flared up, and he felt old for the first time in his career. Alex's eyes blurred as Ivanov sped by. That kid was one hell of a player. Before long, he'd be out on the sidelines, and Ivanov would be the team's light.

This sluggish feeling was why Alex hated drinking and gave it up nearly four years ago. He shouldn't have let his aging ego make him binge again. Plus, his mental health after a night of bingeing always made him depressed. He was getting too old for this life. Thirty-two was their prime to most people, but he was getting up there in hockey. Most of his friends had retired or were about to retire. Emotionally, he felt like he was still in his early to mid-twenties and hated that his body was telling him otherwise. He wasn't ready to let go of this part of his life yet. He had to prove to himself that he was still just as great or greater than he was in his youth.

Alex whistled and motioned with his hand to have the rookies line up so he could show them what he wanted them to work on in their next drill. He had Benson drop the puck, and before Alex could show the men the pass he wanted them to work on, Andreson exploded forward with surprising speed. Within seconds, Alex saw three things: Benson's eyes widened, he motioned his hand for the kid to stop, and shouted, "Not your turn, Anderson." Alex's reflexes slowed from his hangover, and he skated to the side, but his timing was off. A sickening crack echoed through the rink as Alex crumbled to the ice. A loud swear word flew from his mouth as he held the scream in his throat.

Alex lay on the ice, moaning. Benson, Anderson, and the other men hovered around him. Anderson, freaking out, "I'm sorry, I jumped the gun," his voice trailed off.

Moments later, Alex was in the medics office. His knee was being wrapped in a temporary splint as he waited for the ambulance to transport him to the hospital. The ever-stoic Coach Talbot looked pained, and when Alex made eye contact, all he could see was disappointment in the man's eyes. Alex deserved it he screwed up. Alex should have done what coach said and just gone home. If he had, his reflexes would have been better.

The doctor finished wrapping him up. "Well, the bad news is you won't be able to play the rest of the season. The good news is that surgery will fix this, along with some extensive rehab, and before you know it, you will be back in the game."

The doctor stood up and took his leave. Coach Talbot shook his head at the situation and walked the Doctor out. Silence hung heavy in the air at the horrible news.

Benson broke the tension and squeezed Alex's shoulder. "We'll get you back on the ice, Holstead. This isn't over."

Alex managed a weak nod. Shame burned in his eyes as he glanced down at his injured knee, a stark reminder of his reckless behavior last night, trying to act young again. Harsh realities were setting in. "And the season is over," he snapped his fingers, "just like that."

"You'll be back. You've been here before and have always

come back a force to be reckoned with. Just focus on recovery. We'll miss you out there, but we'll hold down the fort."

Alex nodded, but his heart wasn't in it. This time felt different. Last night, he'd been determined to show the newbies how he could dominate, but now it was a lost cause, and there was a huge chance he may never play pro again.

CHAPTER THREE

WHAT'S IN A NAME?

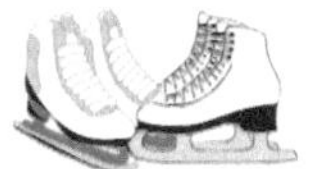

Sarah fidgeted in the crowded Halifax Physiotherapy Clinic waiting room, flipping through a magazine that mocked her with articles about staying positive, moving forward, or the current article, *Finding your soulmate in a sea of fish*. A groan escaped her lips; there was no way she'd ever find her soulmate here. Sarah scanned the waiting area. A group of men brought in a giant Douglas fur, and the office manager pointed to the location near all the boxes of decorations.

Halifax Physiotherapy Clinic was supposed to be the most current and state-of-the-art center for athletes; so far, she only noticed geriatric patients recovering from hip or knee replacements or middle-aged ladies going to the pilates class that just started. So far, the men delivering the tree were the youngest and closest to her age she noticed coming and going.

Sarah glanced at her phone. It was already half past the hour, and her name still hadn't been called. Waiting sucked, and even though she needed the therapy, she didn't feel like wasting her entire morning when Jane was at her apartment. She hadn't seen her best friend in years. They often talked over text, but the best part of their friendship was that they would always pick up where they had left off no matter how long they had been apart or didn't talk.

Fate probably decided to play a joke on Sarah because the only person she could ever claim soulmate to was Jane, her destined soul sister. Sarah glanced down at the article and read a few more paragraphs, frustrated that she was so far behind on the dating scene she couldn't find the interest in half the things the writer was recommending to find you a perfect man.

She didn't want to put herself on a dating site or go to bars. Both of those things made her stomach churn. She wanted to meet someone honest, mindful of their surroundings, and had all their faculties in full function. Meeting someone at a bar who'd been drinking didn't make her feel that safe. That person was their true self. Maybe she was just naive. Perhaps she should do everyday college things, like going to football games or clubbing, or even have a fling just to say she did it.

The door to the therapy room opened, and hoping it was finally her turn, she threw the magazine onto the chair beside her and got her crutches ready to lift her. Unfortunately, it wasn't. A therapist guided another patient who hobbled out with a grimace on their face, noting they had had a tough session and just seeing that made her ankle pulse, knowing what was to come and a cruel reminder of her sluggish recovery. Her life was over, and she couldn't find a silver lining this time.

Suddenly, the door opened, and the air shifted. Sarah shivered and glanced at the entrance. One of the tallest men she'd ever seen walked in. Even with his head hung down and shaggy hair covering his face, he held his broad shoulders back and entered with a confident stride. How did he do that? No matter how often Sarah had to have crutches for injuries, she always seemed to walk awkwardly with them. He looked— graceful. She shook her head. How could a behemoth look graceful?

She made a slight laughing sound. The man turned her way, and she hurriedly turned it into a cough and turned her head away. Her heart leaped into her throat when she got a glimpse of his face. Holy hotcakes, he was the best-looking man she'd ever seen in her entire existence on Earth.

Raw power shot out of his dark blue eyes and jolted right into her stomach. She glanced at him again through the corner of her eye. He scanned the waiting room, and his eyes caught hers again. By all that was holy, he was undeniably handsome, with a rugged jawline, a few day's growth of beard, the manliest man she'd ever seen. Her body shifted in the seat, and she seemed to assess every inch of the man from toe to head, and when she reached his eyes, he was full-on staring at her. That was when she realized he didn't seem too happy with her. His deep blue eyes were squinting in a scowl, and his lips pinched. Was he angry? Annoyed? He turned his back on her, pulled his phone out, and dialed, and she could hear him say, "I thought you said when I got here, it would be empty?"

Sarah turned away, embarrassment oozing out of her. Never in her life had she ogled a man before. It was all Jane and that stupid article's fault for putting ideas into her head. She didn't need a boyfriend to replace skating. She needed to hurry and finish therapy so she could go back home and live her empty life.

She got up and walked awkwardly on her crutches to the reception area. "Excuse me, can you check and see how much longer I need to wait?"

"Name?"

"Sarah Holstead"

The woman at the desk glanced at her computer. Looking flustered, she excused herself for a minute and then returned. "I am so sorry. Your therapist called in sick, and I meant to tell you first, being you were already here, but I jumped the gun and just started canceling her day. But Lindsey said she would fit you in if you are okay with waiting a few more minutes. I think you've had her before."

Sarah didn't care who she had; she just wanted to get the treatment done so she could go home, and she knew it wasn't good to cancel. Even though she was doing the bare minimum, she was still an athlete and knew that if she didn't take care of her ankle, it could make her recovery and life worse in the future. She sighed, "That's fine. I'll wait."

A shiver ran down her spine, a surprising mix of fear and something else. Her heart started racing, and she felt heat emitting from something huge behind her. She turned, and it was the man; he smelled just as divine as his appearance—the same scent of aftershave her grandpa used. The sensation of home and love simultaneously was like having her pulse leap, like doing a triple axle in the air and feeling the wind in her hair.

Still embarrassed from scoping him out and now this reaction, Sarah kept her head down and tried hard to hurry away. Fortunately, the door to the back opened, and Lindsey, her physical therapist, called "Holstead" without looking up from her chart.

Sarah breathed a sigh of relief and was about to follow the woman when a crutch clanked hers right before her, stopping her. Sarah glared at the owner; the large, beautiful man with angry eyes glared at her. Frustrated at this man who made her feel too many things, she blurted out angrily, "She called Holstead."

"Yeah," he replied dryly, "and that would be me."

Lindsey looked up, flustered, when she noticed the man, "Oh my goodness, Mr. Holstead, I'm so sorry! I didn't... I'm here for Sarah." She stammered, her face burning red.

Sarah couldn't help but flash a triumphant smile at the man. His eyes widened, and his mouth made an "O" shape. A thrill coursed through her, finally getting a different reaction from this intimidatingly attractive stranger. And just as she felt satisfaction at standing her imaginary ground, he rolled his eyes, a hint of a smile played on his lips, and said, "Interesting."

Sarah walked to the back. What did that mean? Sure, her name wasn't the most popular in the world. What made that so interesting? Then, it dawned on her that this stranger may be a relative, and her stomach turned sour. How gross was it that the first man she ever ogled might be a relative? Shame and disgust filled her gut. Jane would feel sorry for her, but once everything died down, Sarah knew that Jane would find her predicament funny and tease her mercilessly forever about her first experience acknowledging the opposite sex.

A few minutes later, a booming voice called, "Alex Holstead!" Alex was the gorgeous man's name. She found herself fascinated with him. He stook with a few awestruck patients who'd managed to finagle a few photos and autographs. He didn't seem as angry as he did in the waiting room. His smile lit up his entire face and made her heart thud heavily. She shivered and turned away, wanting to slap her cheek to get her head on straight. They had the same last name; she couldn't drool over a potential relative.

On the zero-gravity treadmill, Sarah overheard one of the older men who took a picture say, "I can't believe I met Alex Holstead! Here of all places." He stopped looking at his phone and put it in his pocket, then told his PT, "For the first time,

I'm glad I had to come to physiotherapy. I wouldn't trade this for anything!"

After her twenty minutes on the treadmill were up, Lindsey returned, and they went to a table to work on ankle rotations. Sarah whispered, "Who's Alex Holstead?"

Lindsey's jaw dropped. "You… don't know? He's the star center for the Halifax Hurricanes! Not to mention, the city's most eligible bachelor!"

Sarah's cheeks flushed. So the ruggedly sexy mystery man was a local celebrity? A sudden, unexpected feeling of excitement bubbled within her, followed once more by dread at the reminder that they had the same name. Lindsey stopped working on Sarah's ankle and said, nearly starstruck, "Do you think you are related, and if so, could you maybe introduce me?"

Sarah felt despondent. Of course, Lindsey would be interested. He was so attractive; how could he not be the most eligible bachelor in the city? "I have no clue if we're related. I've never done a family tree, and where I come from in Louisiana, the only Holsteads in the area are my family, which consists of my Grandpa, mom, and me."

"Well, this might be a prime time for you to make acquaintances and find out. It would be wild if you met a long-lost cousin so far from home."

Sarah felt awkward talking about this but still responded, even if it sounded despondent. "It would."

She did her exercises for the rest of her session and couldn't help but keep looking at Alex. He was all into his therapy session; he had taken his long joggers off and put on a pair of sports shorts. The muscles on his legs were bulging, showing that he used those muscles in skating well. Sarah didn't go for the hockey jocks, they were always so brutish, and she couldn't help but be a bit judgy about their looks.

Half of them didn't have teeth, which honestly freaked her out. She had nightmares about losing teeth.

She shivered at the thought. Alex, though, was smiling every time she glanced his way. He seemed to thrive on exercising his knee, and she couldn't help noting that he had a beautiful, complete set of white teeth.

CHAPTER FOUR

IMPRESSIONS COUNT

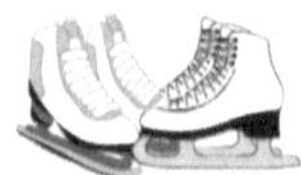

*R*elief washed over Alex as he finally escaped the first few minutes of taking care of his fans. He always tried to treat each one special. If it weren't for his fans and the fans of the Halifax Hurricanes, his bills wouldn't be paid. He respected all the people who spent their hard-earned money for him and his team to entertain them.

Today, though, was suddenly different. A strange lightness had replaced the usual post-surgery doldrums. Alex couldn't grasp it until he spotted the young, defiant blonde beauty across the room. "Interesting," he muttered again.

His physiotherapist Phil looked up, "What was that?"

"Nothing," Alex said clearly. He suddenly felt the urge to work hard and prove to the woman that he wasn't a wuss. "Phil, I want you to work me hard today. I'm ready."

Phil lifted a brow. "I'm not sure. The notes on your chart transfer said you were still not at forty percent."

"That is because I wasn't ready. I can feel it today. I'm ready. I know you can push me. Trust me, I know my body."

Phil assessed Alex, "Alright, if you do well with the first

few exercises, I will push you harder in the second half. Deal?"

Alex nodded, "If that is as good as I will get, that is fine."

The first few stretches hurt like hell. He hadn't been mentally ready for rehab; he was too depressed, thinking he'd have to retire, but for some reason, that little blonde had some sort of energy that shot out of her and right into him. He never wanted to make a woman notice him as much as he wanted her to. She never once looked his way for the first twenty minutes, and if she did, he missed it. Then he heard her therapist call her name and couldn't help but grin.

That was when he noticed her looking at him. She was frowning but had the prettiest flushed cheeks. She reminded him of an ice princess in a fantasy movie. Her hair was either very blonde or died silvery blonde, her nose had the cutest elfish tilt, and her wide eyes the palest of blue, or were they green? He could not quite tell the exact shade from this distance, and the strangest thing was that they shared their last name.

Alex wondered if she spelled it the same, but he knew she wasn't from his hometown of Halifax. No, she was from somewhere magical, and that was undeniably intriguing. Her voice was melodic, and as he listened to her speak from across the room, he heard the soft southern lilt from the American South somewhere.

Even the way she said, "Holstead," sent a shiver down his spine.

She moved from the zero-gravity treadmill to the table. Her therapist was stretching her ankle. He wondered what happened to her. She was fit, and he could tell even in the baggy joggers she had on. Alex wondered if she, too, was an athlete hoping for a more private state-of-the-art facility. Alex found himself smiling despite the pain radiating in his knee.

He was on the stationary bike and felt sweat plaster his hair on his forehead. Would she find that attractive or repulsive? His hair fell over his eyes, and it was the perfect cover for him to keep his eyes on her. Alex caught her staring again, and he couldn't help but grin. Her cheeks turned pink, and she hurriedly turned away. He felt a bubble of laughter emit from his chest, and he tried to stop it from erupting.

She reminded him of a schoolgirl in a woman's face and body. There was a captivating innocence about her, a refreshing contrast to the usual puck bunnies who generally fawned over him.

She also appeared to be utterly oblivious to his stolen glances. The Southern lilt of her voice drifted through the room like a melody, then turned to a whisper. Piqued, Alex strained his ears to see if he could pick up what she and her therapist were whispering about. Her therapist's gaze shifted towards him, then back to the woman. Bingo. She must have been asking about him.

A mischievous grin spread across his face. As her therapist talked, his princess' brow furrowed slightly. Was she annoyed at something the therapist said about him? He found the thought oddly amusing and chuckled out loud. She turned toward him, and her brows scrunched up in what appeared to be annoyance. He smiled wider. Her mouth slightly dropped open, and her eyes looked dreamy, far-off. Then she shook her head and frowned again.

What was his ice princess thinking? Eventually, he noticed something: every time he smiled her way, her eyes sparkled, followed by a comical scrunch of her brow as if she was frustrated that she liked what she saw. That made him work harder.

Alex found a welcome change to the monotony of his recovery. Now, he had to figure out how to get on the same schedule as this woman. He had to know more about her.

The rest of the therapy went by too fast. She was already lying on a table with ice around her ankle for the cool-down. He had to talk to her. He waved over Phil.

"I'm done. I want to go lay over there by that woman with my ice now." Phil didn't hesitate, probably assuming that my title of ladies' man didn't stop me from trying to hook up even in physiotherapy. Even though Alex hated that title, it was because he was always with Benson, who had a girl on each arm, that he ended up getting the reputation.

Alex was a one-woman man, and the last time he had a long-term relationship was when he was in middle school and before focusing on going pro. Could you even consider that a relationship? The other women were just fillers until he retired and decided to settle down and start a family, which he planned on doing when he was closer to forty. But this was the first time in years that he wanted to get to know someone, and he wouldn't let the opportunity go by without giving it a shot.

Whenever Alex sat down, an involuntary groan of pain came out, and he sighed so much for looking strong in front of his ice princess. He sounded like an old man just then. It was an unfortunate reminder that early retirement because of his age and injury was right around the corner. Plus, Ivanov was only twenty-one, and with a bit more practice and a few games with the triple-A, he'd be better than Alex. He should give it all up and leave in glory rather than an old man who lost his game.

She had her arm over her eyes but spoke in that southern lilt he was falling in love with. "I recognize that sound. It's the sigh of feeling defeated." She moved her arm and turned her head towards him.

Alex was shocked at her accurate observation. "How do you know it's defeat and not relief that my session is over?"

She asked. "Is that what it is?"

He sighed. "No. In fact, you are spot on."

"Figured." A grin of satisfaction spread across her lips, and he was mesmerized. Her smile lit up her face, and he decided her eyes were both blue and green. They changed colors with her expressions.

He couldn't stop looking at her and wanted to hear her speak again, "What gave it away?"

"Your body language was screaming it out loud and clear. I've been watching you …"

He could not believe she admitted it and acknowledged it without blushing. He wondered if she even realized what she said.

"… and can tell you are putting much effort into your rehabilitation. You are overworking because you're rushing to get back to the ice. I know that feeling well. You remind me of myself trying to prove to yourself that you are good enough, but your body is telling you that it isn't, and it sucks."

He had to admit she was right and wrong. He wanted to prove himself, but for some strange reason, it was for her, not his team. At the same time, the moment he felt his pained knee with the ice, he thought about losing his career. Frustrated, this little slip of a woman could read him so well ticked him off. How could he have taken all the secret looks as flirting when, in all actuality, she was secretly assessing his inability to get back to the ice? "Well, gee, that makes me feel all warm and fuzzy. Are you telling me that I am too old and need to pack my bags because my time in the limelight is over? If so, that's a pretty crappy thing to tell a person who's down and out already."

She shifted. "You're testy, aren't you? I was just pointing out that I get it from one athlete to another."

Alex sighed. "So, it wasn't an insult? Was it supposed to be consolation?"

"I didn't mean it as an insult nor consolation. It was just an observation. So what happened to you?" She asked.

"Training the new guys, and ended up in the wrong place at the wrong time. One of the new kids jumped the gun and swung his hockey stick back with all his force to hit the puck, but the backhanded swing bashed into my knee. I had to have surgery."

She cringed. "Ah, sorry. That sucks!"

"Agreed. So, what's your story?"

"I was on my way to the World Championships. I was getting tired and sloppy while practicing my routine and aiming for six quads. When I landed, I busted my ankle again." Sarah wiggled her toes under the ice pack.

Alex chuckled and muttered, "She is an ice princess."

She sat up fast, "What did you just call me?"

"I didn't call you anything."

"You said I was an ice princess. If I'm an ice princess, you are an ice prince."

He burst out laughing. "Ice prince," he spit out, wiping his eyes. "That is a new one. What exactly is that?"

She crossed her arms over her chest. "A cold-hearted jerk."

He could swear she was pouting. She was adorable. "I think you misunderstood. Ice princess isn't an insult; it's just that you remind me of a princess from a fantasy land. You are beautiful."

Her cheeks flamed red, and he could see her chest rise and fall, taking deep, controlled breaths. She opened her mouth as if she were going to say something, and then her teeth clicked shut. She started fidgeting with the ice pack near her ankle.

Alex had never met a woman like her before; she looked absolutely flustered. Had no one ever told this woman she was beautiful, she had to know. He had never met a woman embarrassed by a compliment. Generally, the puck bunnies he dated here and there ate up compliments.

Her timer went off, and she sat up. Alex rushed to sit up and groaned when he pulled his knee.

"You okay?" her embarrassment vanished, and in its place was concern.

"Yeah, you were right. I think I overdid it today."

She gave him a thin-lipped smile and held her hand out to him. "Let's start over. Hi, I'm Sarah Holstead, and you are?"

He smiled. Sarah truly was charming. Instead of shaking her hand, he turned it and did what he'd seen gentlemen of the past do: He brought the top of her hand to his lips and kissed the smooth skin. "Alex Holstead. Nice to meet you."

Sarah grabbed her crutches and left the exercise area without another word. What a morning, this whole situation, this shared name, this sudden burst of sunshine in his otherwise dull day – it was all strangely delightful.

As he headed out, he went to the scheduling counter, flirted a bit with the receptionist, and got all his future appointments rearranged to be with Sarah. He couldn't wait to see what other surprises future encounters with Sarah Holstead would bring.

CHAPTER FIVE

COFFEE AND HOCKEY HOTTIES

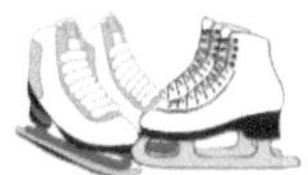

A crisp December breeze nipped at their cheeks, and Christmas was in the air. The streets were all decorated with garland, holly, and twinkling lights. She generally loved this time of year, but ever since meeting Alex, she has started to wish she had someone she could spend it with besides family and friends.

"It's so beautiful here at Christmas," Jane said.

"It is," Sarah said without conviction in her tone. Jane nudged her with her shoulder.

"Well, hopefully, when we return to your rental, the owner will have finished the Christmas decorations, and we can spend my last night enjoying the beginning of the season together."

Sarah breathed, puffed out, and linked arms with Jane, "Yes, and it feels good to be in a boot finally and hang out with you more outside the apartment. I just wish you could stay longer."

Jane lifted her scarf above her nose with her free hand. "Me too, but honestly, although it's beautiful, I never considered how cold it is this far north and near the ocean. For some reason, I thought it wouldn't be this cold." She shivered again.

Sarah chuckled, "Well, in just twenty-four hours, you will be on a plane heading back to what you told me: Seventy-five degrees."

Jane nodded and shivered again when the wind whipped them. With chattering teeth, she said, "I've decided I will take the heat over cold any day of the week. All I need is a good A/C, and I'll be just fine."

They laughed as they walked up the steps to the historic building that looked right out of a Norman Rockwell Christmas postcard. It housed Sarah's favorite coffee shop in her neighborhood. They placed their order and sat at the table. The warmth of having Jane with her in Canada to celebrate American Thanksgiving still lingered in her heart, and her eyes welled up. "I'm going to miss you so much. I wish you didn't have to leave."

Jane unwound her scarf and leaned back in her chair. "Don't make me cry." She sniffed and took a sip of her hot mocha. "This will be a memory that stays in my heart forever. I can't believe I got to see snow—real snow!"

Sarah chuckled, "Honestly, it's rare for it to snow this time of year in Halifax, so I guess you got a Thanksgiving miracle."

The chatter in the coffee shop was getting louder, so Jane sat up straight and leaned forward with a huge grin. "Okay, enough about me leaving and the weather. Tell me what you plan to do about Mr. Hockey Hottie!"

Sarah winced at the nickname but couldn't suppress the smile that tugged at her lips. Three physical therapy sessions with Alex had revealed a surprisingly deep connection. They shared a love for superhero movies and action films, and both had a competitive streak that manifested in their rehab exercises. But their biggest thing in common was the profound respect for each other's struggles. Yet, a knot of confusion sat heavy in Sarah's stomach. She was falling hard and fast but didn't want to. She didn't know him well enough yet. What if he was like a first cousin or something? She'd only seen him three times. How could she fall for someone that fast? She shivered, and her stomach churned at her reaction to him. She pushed her coffee further towards Jane.

"What is going on in that head of yours?" Jane asked.

"He... Alex is complicated," Sarah admitted as she twisted her napkin. "We have a lot in common, but..."

"But what?" Jane pressed, leaning closer. "Does he look at you like one of his puck bunnies?" She wiggled her eyebrows suggestively.

Sarah blushed. "No, not at all! Thank goodness, I don't want to be a groupie. But... I don't know. He called me beautiful the first day, but it feels more like he sees me as a little sister he needs to protect than..." She trailed off, frustration coloring her voice.

"Than a potential girlfriend?" Jane finished, her eyes wide. "Girl, you're overthinking this! First, have you even asked him about the whole last name thing? Maybe there's a Canadian Holstead clan you never knew about!"

Sarah knew that talking to him was the most logical solution, but she thought that just having a workout buddy was all she needed. She didn't know her heart would fall so fast for someone. "You're right, Jane! I should ask him, but..." *What if he was related or worse, not related and just didn't like her as a woman?*

"But nothing!" Jane cut in, her voice firm. "This is Alex Holstead, hockey superstar and your potential soulmate, right? Don't let him slip away because of some silly what-ifs. Besides," she leaned in conspiratorially, "this is the first guy you've ever talked about, Sarah! Not even little Noah from first grade held a candle to this much conversation about boys between us!"

Sarah swatted Jane's arm playfully, a laugh escaping her lips. "Okay, okay! You win. I'll ask him. But if it turns out we're long-lost cousins…"

"Then you can move on with a clear conscience," Jane finished, winking. "But seriously, Sarah, this could be something amazing. Don't let fear hold you back."

Sarah took a deep breath, the warmth of the coffee spreading through her. Maybe Jane was right. Maybe it was time to take a chance and see where this unexpected connection with Alex could lead. After all, with Christmas just around the corner, a little holiday magic might be exactly what she needed.

Sarah sat on her sofa, Christmas music playing over the speakers, a fire roaring in the fireplace, and daydreaming about Alex when her phone rang. She picked it up, and her heart thumped frantically against her ribs. It was Alex.

"Hello," Her voice wavered.

"Hey Sarah, Benson talked me into getting off my ass and to the home game tonight. I know it's last minute, but I'd love for you to come with me and check out the Hurricanes?" That simple question sent waves of conflicting emotions crashing over her.

When she said nothing, his voice hitched into a more sales pitch, "Seats are behind the bench. Getting that close for an outsider is rare. Will you come? I want to show you what I do."

Her mind raced. Sitting rink-side, practically amongst Alex's team, the Halifax Hurricanes, was an offer that sent shivers of excitement down her spine. But a knot of apprehension tightened in her stomach, too. Meeting his teammates, these larger-than-life hockey figures, was intimidating.

Taking a deep breath, Sarah remembered Jane's pep talk from earlier. "Be yourself, Sarah." Besides, this might be her best chance to ask Alex about their shared last name – a question that had been gnawing at her since their first encounter.

"Sarah, are you there?" Alex's voice wavered now.

Sarah cleared her throat. "Hey, yeah, sorry, I'm here." She took a deep breath, and with a newfound resolve, she finally answered him. "Yeah, that sounds like fun. I'll meet you there." And she hung up on him before he could say anything, or she lost her nerve.

A nervous flutter filled her stomach as she took extra care to get ready. She curled her hair, put on makeup, wore her skin-tight jeans, and found a floral silk top in Halifax Hurricanes colors of orange, blue, and gold. Tonight wasn't just about hockey. It was an opportunity to get closer to Alex, see how he introduced her to his hockey family, gauge his interest, and hopefully unravel the mystery of their last name.

The cab dropped her off, and she hobbled to the ticket booth. "I'm supposed to meet Alex Holstead. Did he leave me tickets?"

"Name." The man looked her up and down, handed her the ticket, and gave her a weird expression.

He probably thought she was his long-lost sister or something. What was she thinking? There was no way this was a date. He just wanted her to meet his buddies, all the people he'd been talking about in physical therapy. The entryway into the arena had an enormous twelve-foot Christmas tree in the center, and all the decorations were hockey sticks, pucks, and Halifax Hurricane team jerseys with each member's number. She searched the tree for Alex's number, Fifty Two, which he told her he picked because it was his dad's football number back in high school, and took a selfie beside it.

The crowded arena buzzed with energy, and the deafening roar momentarily washed away her anxieties. The team must have come out the back, and she hurriedly made her way through the crowd to search for the Hurricanes box. It took a while, but she finally spotted Alex. He was leaning against the back wall in the bench area for his team, and he was even wearing his jersey.

Concern laced her brow. Alex's knee had not healed yet, and his coach seriously couldn't think of letting him play. He looked up, his face lighting up with a smile that crinkled the corners of his eyes when he saw her, and her fears vanished.

"There you are!" he boomed, his voice easily reaching her over the cacophony. "Come on, I saved you a spot."

He stepped out of the box, wearing jeans and his jersey, and thank goodness he wasn't in gear. He kissed her cheek, "I'm so glad you made it." He grabbed her hand and laced his fingers in hers. A bolt of joy raced through her, and she smiled and giddily laughed as they hobbled through a maze of equipment bags and burly hockey players, their greetings ranging from curious to playful to slapping on Alex's butt with wolf whistles. Sarah plastered on a smile, feeling like a tiny boat navigating a sea of giants but couldn't help being overjoyed at the welcome. They sat down on the bench with some of the younger team members, and Sarah leaned in and whispered in Alex's ear. "When you said behind the bench, I didn't realize you meant where the team sat. I was thinking more like box seats." She pointed to the glass boxes above the arena.

He smiled and squeezed her hand, still clasped tight in his hand and now resting on his thigh. "This is better. It's where all the action is off the ice.

Sarah felt so small next to all these men. Worried that the team would get her opinion wrong, she hurriedly removed her hand from his and sat on them. Alex stood up and started to jest and interact with the behemoths on the team pre-game. As she watched, her nerves began to get the better of her. Maybe she was delusional, thinking she fit in with him. Suddenly, Sarah wanted to shrink into herself to avoid being seen. Technically, as Sarah stood up behind Alex, she noticed that at five foot three and with her waif-like body, she was the same width as Alex's thigh, and if she stood sideways, she would appear as if she vanished from the rest of the team's sight.

If she thought Alex was huge, the man who appeared next to him made her feel even smaller. That man could snap her in half like a twig. The giant smiled and had so many missing teeth that Sarah sucked her lips in, thanking god that her profession didn't cause teeth loss. She had way too many nightmares that all her teeth would fall out. She didn't know how the hockey players didn't seem to mind or care that they didn't have any.

The giant grabbed Alex and placed his head under his arm, giving him a nuggie. "Holstead, you came!" Then, the giant notices Sarah.

"Ah, is this the little figure skater you've been on about?"

The flutters of wings went wild inside of her. Alex talked about her. She smiled and nodded. The big guy put his hand out, "Troy Benson, the sexiest member of the team. When you get sick of this loser, you can call me."

Sarah felt her cheeks heat. Alex shoved her hand out of

Benson's. "Don't mess with her, Benson. I wanted to give her a good impression of the team."

The team started chatting about the game, and Ivanov asked Alex for some last-minute advice. The first timer rang, letting the audience know the game was about to begin, when Alex knocked on a young player's head that was down. The young man looked up, and Alex said, "You better have been training hard, rookie. I expect to see that speed on the ice moving that puck for a win."

The kid nodded, "I'm really sorry, man. I'm glad you're back, even if it's not to play."

That must have been the guy who had injured Alex, Sarah thought. Then Alex stepped to the side and pulled her out. "I'm sure you are all wondering who this little beauty is, and I'm surprised Benson hasn't told any of you…" Alex grabbed her hand. "This is," he kissed her on the top of her hand, "Sarah Holstead."

All the team started hooting, and the big redheaded giant with no teeth kneeled in front of her and bowed. "How the hell did you tie this bachelor down in—" he looked up to Alex, "Dude, you've only been gone three months." The man then looked at Sarah's flat stomach. "Is there a little nudger on the way?"

So, he never told Benson her last name. That was interesting.

Once more, the team started clicking their sticks and stomping their skates on the wood. Sarah knew that her cheeks were flaming red because they burned like fire, and all Alex did was laugh. Was this why he wanted her to come to play a joke on the guys? That was so not nice, and she tugged her hand out of his grasp.

She put her hands on her hips and looked up angrily at everyone, "I am not pregnant, and I am not married to this buffoon. For your information, we've only been in physical therapy together for a few weeks and discovered we shared the same last name. If anything," she looked him up and down, "he's first too big for my taste and way too old for me. I'm only twenty-two."

Sarah noticed Alex frowning. Then she scanned the team and found the cutest and probably the shortest player. She pointed at Jenö and said, "It would be more appropriate to say I would be better suited to him."

Benson whistled as he got up. "You're a little spitfire. Hey Jenö, it looks like you might have a new fan."

Sarah's ego was bruised. She rolled her eyes and put her arms over her chest. Alex played her, and she felt like a fool. She had really liked him but struggled with the internal dilemma of finding out if he was related. Now Sarah knew he wasn't interested and just wanted to mess with the team. Tonight was definitely not a date as she had imagined, and she wished she hadn't tried to make herself look pretty before leaving. She should have come with no makeup and her grungy sweats. With her shoulders straight and standing at her full height, she said, "I am here as a courtesy to my PT partner. Hockey is not my thing. I much rather the more graceful art of figure skating."

The coach blew his whistle. "No more small talk. Holstead's take-a-seat games about to start." Then he called out the players to get on the ice.

Sarah turned to Alex. "That wasn't very nice. You embarrassed me. If you had told me you wanted to play a joke, I wouldn't have minded playing along."

Alex smiled but looked contrite. "Honestly, I didn't intend to do that; it sort of just happened, but I have to admit seeing all their faces was priceless."

Sarah sighed. She didn't want to stay mad at him. Sitting quietly momentarily, they watched the puck drop and the game start. She knocked her shoulder into his, "I have to admit, Benson bowing to me was pretty funny."

Alex laughed. "It was perfect. Sorry that his head is always in the gutter. I don't like that he would think I'd take advantage of you that fast."

Sarah felt her cheeks flush again. That fast? Did that mean he wanted to take advantage of her slower? She bit her tongue, trying to get her mind out of the gutter, and forced herself to focus on the game. As the Hurricanes played, she didn't talk to Alex. Most of the time, Alex stood banging on the window, separating the bench from the ice, cursing out different players.

Although Sarah had never been to a hockey game before, she started getting the hang of it and found it rather exciting. She was shocked by their dexterity with their footwork on the ice under so much pressure and with all the padded accessories. No wonder why they needed to be big and strong. She watched their footwork and noticed the differences between them and figure skaters. They had speed and used their calves more in how they used their skates.

Sarah jumped up as Ivanov went down from the opposing team, whacking him over the head with his stick. She slammed her hand against the glass and shouted, "Foul play! "

Alex and the other team members on the bench called "Penalty."

Within seconds, a fight occurred when Benson shoved the guy who purposely hit Ivanov.

Alex started shouting, "Back off, Benson," the big redhead either heard or quit on his own because he spit on the guy and went back to check on Ivanov.

Sarah turned to Alex. "Hockey is a dangerous sport. I had no idea. No wonder all of you are such big men." She watched how the team just kept playing. No time outs or anything.

"Why didn't they pull that guy out? Or give y'all a timeout?"

"That happens often," Alex pointed to the other team. He got benched, so they have to play one man short until the timer stops."

"Wow. That was dumb of him."

"Yeah, but good for us. Now we have a better chance of getting some big scores."

"Alex," Sarah began, leaning closer to be heard over the game, "about the whole Holstead thing…"

Alex chuckled a low rumble that sent shivers down her spine. "Do you know anything about your ancestry?"

He winked, "Intrigued, are we?"

"Extremely," she admitted, her voice barely a whisper. "I need to know if there's any chance…"

The roar of the crowd drowned her out. Alex jumped up, cheering. The Hurricanes just scored for the win. Even though Alex had his knee in a brace and was still recovering, he picked her up and spun her around. His blue eyes sparkled with amusement.

His lips brushed her ear."We'll talk about it later, but first, it's time to celebrate!"

Alex placed her down and congratulated his team. He lifted Ivanov, his replacement, and spun the big man the same way. The entire team raced to his side to stop him. Alex laughed it all off.

Sarah couldn't help but smile. Maybe the truth about their last name could wait. Tonight, she would lose herself in the electrifying energy of the win and the undeniable thrill of being next to Alex Holstead, famous Pro Hockey player, in his element.

Alex was buzzing. The Hurricane won, but the best part of the night was seeing Sarah get into the game. She was a spitfire, even though she didn't know about any of the terms. She got heated at the exact times he had. Tonight, she finally broached the topic of their shared name. He wanted her to be the first to talk about it. That way, he would know if what they shared was flirting or her being a Southern sweetheart.

Luckily, her grandpa called during their second physiotherapy session, and Alex saw George Holstead flash on the screen. He tucked that piece of knowledge away and later that day went to his dad and searched their Geneology charts for hours, searching to make sure there was zero connection or, if any, a very far-off relative, so far off it would be as if they were strangers. Fortunately, his dad had worked on their family tree for over thirty years and had a list of ancestors all the way back to five times removed, and George Holstead from Louisiana wasn't among them. It was just a small world where he met another person with his name and exact spelling.

At the bar, he couldn't stop looking at Sarah as he talked to his teammates, joking and laughing as if she'd known them her entire life. She sipped her drink and, caught him staring, and winked at him. His mind went back to earlier that night when the Hurricanes won, and he spun Sarah around, ignoring the twinge in his knee and her fingers playing with the back of his hair at his neck. Then, when her lithe body slid down him, a fire burned so deep inside of him that he wanted to kiss her. Her cheeks had been flushed, her eyes bright with excitement, and her lips rosy. And now, watching her interact with his friend and knowing they were not related, his heart swelled in anticipation. The feeling in his gut for Sarah was more intense than any pre or post-game thrill. He never felt this with a woman before, and he knew that Sarah was the one.

While looking at the ancestry documents, Alex had asked his father how long it took him to fall for his mom, and his dad told him he knew his mother was the one for him the moment they met. He said he felt it in his gut. Alex figured the knowing must be a Holstead trait because the second Sarah glanced his way again, with her cheeks flushed and her colossal smile, he felt the chemistry between them burn. He grinned back at her, stalked towards her, and leaned in, "Having a good time?"

She nodded, "Your team is awesome. Now I understand why you feel like a family. I wish my figure skating team had been like this instead of always feeling like we were competitors."

He wrapped his arm around her waist and squeezed it. "It must have been lonely."

"It was, but I don't need to worry about that anymore."

She looked both sad and happy, and all he wanted to do was kiss her. So, before he lost all his senses, he said, "Let's get a cab and head out. Maybe we can get a coffee before heading home."

Sarah turned in his arms, "Or we can drink some coffee at my place?"

She looked up at him so innocently that he had no idea if she knew what she was asking, but he wasn't about to deny her wish. He wanted to make sure she understood one very important thing. "By the way, I looked up our ancestry; we aren't related."

Sarah's mouth made a little "O." Her eyes widened, and her cheeks turned flame-red. She leaned into him, kissed his chest through his jersey, and swayed a bit. "That is good news because I really like you." She poked him in the chest, which she just kissed. I mean really like you, like you. I've never liked anyone before; you are the first."

Alex smiled down at her. "Let's get you home. I think the alcohol is gone to your head."

She slapped her chest over her heart. "No, it's right here. My heart hasn't stopped beating since I met you. I want to be with you. Will you be with me?" She then gave him puppy-dog eyes and pouted her lip.

"Once you're sober, if you still feel that way, I will definitely be with you."

He helped her outside and hailed a cab. She gave the address to her apartment, and he helped her inside. She kicked off her shoes at the door and started taking off her clothes one by one, and he froze. She was playing a dangerous game, but he couldn't take advantage. Not tonight.

She turned around, "Are you coming?" she walked to her bedroom. He thought the ball was in her park and the real game was about to begin, but now the tables were turned, and he knew he should reign it back in. Sarah wasn't a puck bunny; she was going to be his. But would that be tonight, or should he wait? His brain was foggy from the alcohol he consumed, and he couldn't decide what he should do. Without thinking, he followed her into the bedroom, taking his jersey off as he went.

CHAPTER SIX

WHAT DID I DO?

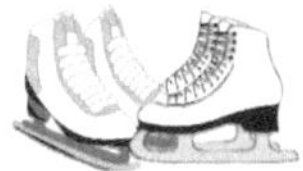

Sarah woke up with her head pounding. She drank way to much last night. Honestly she never drank that much in her life, she always restricted herself from drinking, but the team kept buying her drinks that tasted like punch with a kick and after a while she didn't even taste the kick anymore. She held her hands to her head and tried to remember how she even got home until she heard clanking in the kitchen.

She threw the covers back, then back on just as fast when she was only wearing her bra and panties and started mumbling "oh no" repeatedly. She pulled the comforter off the bed and wrapped herself in it and ran to the bathroom. Looking in the mirror she looked a mess. Her blonde hair was a nest, her eye liner smudged down to her cheeks, and her eyes blood shot.

Grabbing her phone she dialed Jane. It took two rings before Jane answered. "I've only been gone twenty-four hours. You miss me already?" She said jovially.

Sarah whispered, "I got drunk for the first time in my life

and woke up in my bra and panties and someone is in my kitchen and it smells like bacon is cooking."

The squeal on the other side of the phone made Sarah's head hurt worse. "Shhh, my head feels like it wants to explode."

"Is it Mr. Hockey Hottie?"

"I can only assume it is. I've not made it into the kitchen yet. Jane, I have no recall of what I did, only flashes of me taking my clothes off. I am not that girl; why am I that girl when drunk? He is going to look at me differently. Now he is going to think I'm just another puck bunny."

Jane took pity on Sarah. "No, he won't y'all have something in common compared to those women. First of all, you understand the hard work and dedication to your profession, and you can skate circles around those hockey players. Don't forget you and Alex also shared what it's like to be out injured and how hard that is emotionally."

"True," Sarah muttered. "But what if I took advantage of him? I really like him, Jane, and if I did now he knows and I still don't know if he's related or not. How sick am I?"

"You aren't sick but you do need to take an aspirin , hop into the shower, then go talk to him. I am certain that from what you told me about him that he wouldn't let you take advantage of him nor would he take advantage of you."

"I guess I have no other choice, do I?"

Jane laughed, "Not unless you want to jump out the window to escape." A loud clang came from the background of Jane's phone. "Sorry, Sarah, I have to go. I've been staying with Aunt Matilda, helping her out, and she is driving me nuts. She can't remember anything anymore and keeps thinking the baking dishes go on the stairs, and she tries to sled down on them. Thank goodness I put up a booby trap to stop her before she hurts herself."

Sarah hung up and followed Jane's suggestion of taking

aspirin and a shower. By the time she was out, her head felt clearer. Now it was time to face the consequences of her actions, and made a silent vow to never drink like that again because she hated feeling like this.

With her hair in a ponytail and dressed in a black turtleneck and loose-flowing pants, she headed into the kitchen. Alex was wearing the same clothes from last night and humming as he flipped pancakes. Sarah hesitated at the entry and watched him. He seemed happy, and it didn't seem like he was mad at her.

Alex spotted her, and he grinned. "Good Morning! How are you feeling this morning?"

"I've had better mornings," Sarah said shyly with her hands in the deep pockets of her pants.

Alex, ever the gentleman, took her cue and focused on the pancakes. "Not sure about you, but I like to have a good, greasy breakfast after a night of drinking, so I went to the market down the street and cooked. I hope you don't mind."

Sarah shook her head. "I just wanted you to know I rarely drink. Honestly, that was the first time I had ever been to a bar. The most alcohol I've ever had was a glass of wine on my twenty-first birthday, and my coach insisted it was a rite of passage. I generally don't drink because I don't want to ever be out of control with my skating."

Alex didn't say anything but handed her a mug of coffee. Sarah kept her head down, looking at the mug, and noticed the color was correct. She took a sip, which was exactly the right amount of vanilla creamer. She was amazed that he remembered what she liked after only watching her make coffee at PT while waiting for their appointment.

The image of her trying to lure him to her room filled her with shame. "I am so sorry about last night. I..."

Alex interrupted and lifted her chin with his finger to look at him. "You did nothing to be ashamed of. I took you home, helped you to bed, and slept on the couch. We both had a bit too much to drink, but I want you to know I would never take advantage of you. When you are ready for the next level of our relationship, I am more than open to it."

Sarah's heart fluttered. "Our relationship? But what if we are related?"

Alex's grin grew. "We aren't. I did my research. I went to my dad. He has our entire family tree back to the sixteen hundreds, and you are not part of my ancestry; it's just a wild coincidence."

Sarah jumped up and ran into the kitchen, hugging him. Laughing, he picked her up and spun her around. Before Sarah knew what was happening, his lips were on her still smiling lips, and a jolt of shock ran down her spine. Her first kiss, she froze and stiffened. Alex pulled his head back and set her down. "I am so sorry, I thought."

Sarah knew her face was beet red, and her cheeks burned. "I—uh." She bit her lip and swallowed. "Um, it just took me by surprise," she started, stepping side to side, and embarrassment flooded her at what she was about to admit to him. He was so much older, and she knew he had a ton of relationships; after all, he was the most eligible Batchelor on his team.

Her voice came out barely a whisper. "That was my first kiss, and I didn't know how to react. It's my fault, not yours."

"You kidding," Alex said, sounding shocked. When Sarah couldn't lift her head for fear he would laugh, she felt his finger under her chin, forcing her to look up at him. "Sarah, would you mind if I kissed you?" He asked.

Sarah nodded, tilted her head to him this time, and closed her eyes. It felt like it was taking him forever, and she peeped one eye open. He was just looking at her. "What am I doing wrong?"

Alex chuckled. "No, it's just been a long time since I've

dated someone so innocent. I wanted to savor the moment. You make me feel young again."

Sarah reacted with a light slap on his arm. "You are not old. Thirty-two is still young, so stuff it. When you talk like you're old, it creeps me out."

She crossed her arms when he laughed. "I'm serious. It's gross thinking you think you're old and like me when I'm twenty-two. Ten years isn't that big a deal." She then grabbed a plate and started piling food on it, losing the opportunity for another kiss.

Alex couldn't believe his luck meeting such an extraordinary woman. Last night, he took everything he had not to give in to her, and now that he knew Sarah had never been kissed, he was definitely glad he had better sense, even when drunk, not to give into his baser needs.

She was beyond extraordinary; this was the first time in his life that he wanted to take things slow and learn each other. All he wanted to do was spend time with her, and now he would make an extra effort to show her that he is more than the typical playboy that his past has turned him into. He was going to treat her like what she was: a treasure.

They ate in silence as he considered how to stay with her longer. His phone dinged with an update for his team regarding some of the functions that the team was donating time. Alex was exempt because of his recovery, but that didn't mean the list wasn't perfect for him to woo Sarah. The list had every Christmas event in Halifax listed, and this was the perfect time of year for romance.

CHAPTER SEVEN

CAN LIFE GET ANY MORE PERFECT?

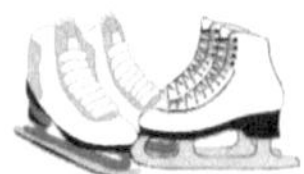

The day flew by, and Alex wasn't ready for it to end. Sarah was in her kitchen unloading her dishwasher.

"Sarah," Alex said as he watched her.

She looked up, "yeah?"

"Would you like to go to the Christmas Market with me this evening?"

Her face lit up. "Like a date?"

Was it like a date? Yes, he wanted her. He wanted more than a fling, and he'd been thinking about this all day. Why did he rush to find out if they were related if he wasn't interested in more? He made up his mind. He was doing this because he wanted to date her, screw their age difference. In so many ways, she was innocent, but in others, she was more mature than he was, and reverse for him, he was very worldly in many ways but immature in others. Their emotional ages ended up meeting in the middle, which was perfect for him, and he hoped she would think the same.

"Yes, Sarah, would you go on a date with me?"

"Absolutely. Are you ready to go, or do I need to change?"

Alex laughed with relief. "No, you are perfect, but if you don't mind, I'd like to go to my place and shower and change. I still smell like a bar."

"True, you do stink." She playfully pinched her nose.

Alex got up and gathered his jacket, "I will come back to pick you up. I am released to drive again."

"That is fantastic. Congratulations, and hurry back."

Alex left, took a shower, and changed so fast. He was back at Sarah's within the hour, knocking on her door.

When Sarah opened it, she had put on makeup and a cute hat with a large pompom on top. She was beautiful and cute all at once. She was laughing and pinched him playfully on his abdomen and said, "Twinsies."

Alex rubbed the slight sting from her pinch and gave her a crooked grin. "What are we in middle school again?"

"Hey!" she playfully slapped his arm. Twinsies is ageless, and you dressed just like me, so I couldn't ignore it."

Alex looked down at what he thought he randomly pulled out of his closet and made a noncommittal sound. Instead of dwelling on his fashion choices, he grabbed her hand.

"Ready to go?" without waiting for her reply, he led her to the car.

It took less than ten minutes to get to the Christmas Market. He opened the car door for Sarah, and they headed into the market, where the crisp December air nipped at their cheeks. Twinkling lights adorned every stall, casting a warm glow on the festive scene. The aroma of roasted chestnuts and spiced cider hung heavy in the air, mingling with the joyous carols emanating from a nearby stage.

Sarah's eyes sparkled like the fairy lights overhead, taking in the sights and sounds with childlike wonder. Every few steps, she'd stop to marvel at a handcrafted ornament or squeal with delight at the sight of a fluffy reindeer puppet. Alex couldn't help but smile at her infectious enthusiasm. He found himself forgetting about the age difference, the uncertainty of the night before melting away in the warmth of her presence.

"This is amazing!" Sarah exclaimed, stopping to admire a stall overflowing with colorful knitted scarves. "I don't think I've ever seen a Christmas market this magical."

Alex chuckled, his gaze lingering on her. "It's not bad, is it?" He reached out, gently tucking a stray strand of hair behind her ear. The simple touch sent a shiver down her spine.

"It's perfect," she whispered, cheeks flushing a delicate pink.

Sarah picked up two scarves and checked them out. "I'm going to mail these to my Grandpa. As he gets older, the few cold days back home are rough on him. These should keep him extra warm."

Alex held the bag for her, and they continued their stroll, hand in hand, weaving through the crowd. Alex playfully teased her about having the same terrible taste in holiday sweaters – a matching pair of garish reindeer designs they'd spotted. The shared laughter only deepened their connection when Alex bought them the pair, and they put them on immediately.

At one stall, Sarah spotted a personalized ornament booth. Her eyes gleaming, she pulled Alex towards it.

"Can we get one?" she pleaded, tugging on his arm.

"Sure," Alex agreed, a smile playing on his lips.

As they picked out their ornaments – a miniature hockey stick for Alex and a dainty snowflake for Sarah – a comfortable silence settled between them. It wasn't awkward but rather a cozy space filled with unspoken emotions.

The man etching their names onto the ornaments chuckled. "Young love, eh?"

Sarah and Alex exchanged a shy glance.

"Actually," Alex started, clearing his throat, "this is our first date."

"Ah," the man winked. "Well, let's hope this market brings you a little Christmas magic and this be the first of many."

They thanked the man and walked away, the inscription on their ornaments a tangible reminder of this special evening.

Sarah and Alex finished their Christmas shopping for all their family and friends, and as the night deepened, they found themselves drawn towards the sound of laughter. A group of carollers sang with gusto, their joyful voices echoing through the square. Sarah and Alex joined in, singing along to the familiar tunes, their voices blending perfectly.

As the last carol faded, Sarah turned to Alex, her eyes sparkling with warmth. "Thank you for this," she said softly. "It's been a night I won't forget."

Alex took a deep breath, his heart pounding in his chest. "Me neither, Sarah." He leaned in closer, their faces inches apart. "Can... I kiss you?"

His voice was a low rumble, sending goosebumps erupting on her skin. Sarah hesitated momentarily, her heart skipping a beat, and the undeniable spark between them erased any remaining doubts.

With a shy smile, she nodded.

As their lips met, the world around them seemed to fade away. The kiss was tender, full of promise and unspoken feelings. When they finally pulled apart, breathless and slightly dazed, Sarah couldn't help but grin.

"Maybe this Christmas market does bring a little magic," she whispered, leaning into him again.

Alex held her close, a newfound hope blossoming in his heart. This unlikely encounter, sparked by a drunken confession and a morning of unexpected intimacy, might lead to something beautiful. And under the twinkling lights of the Christmas market, surrounded by the spirit of the season, anything seemed possible.

The morning light streamed through Sarah's window, painting warm stripes across the room. She curled up on the couch, the phone pressed to her ear. "Jane, you won't believe it!" Sarah practically vibrated with excitement as she cradled her phone between her ear and shoulder, a mug of steaming coffee clutched in her other hand.

"Spill it, girl!" Jane's voice crackled through the line, "Did you finally talk to Mr. Hockey Hottie about the whole Holstead thing?" Jane's voice crackled with excitement from across the line.

"Yes. He did all the research, and we are not related!"

Jane squealed so loud that she pulled the phone away from her ear, laughing.

"But that isn't why I called," Sarah admitted, a playful smile tugging at her lips.

"Oh my gosh, did you..." Jane let her thoughts hang.

"No! Alex asked me on a real date."

Being the absolute best friend, Jane squealed again in joy for Sarah. "Tell me everything."

She recounted the entire Christmas market date, her voice animated as she described the twinkling lights, the delicious smells, and Alex's surprisingly good taste in holiday sweaters, which they wore immediately.

Jane listened intently, punctuating Sarah's narration with

excited gasps and squeals. "Oh my gosh, Sarah! The matching ornaments, the caroling, the..." Jane's voice dropped to a whisper,

Sarah cut her off, a blush creeping up her cheeks. "But Jane, when we were singing carols together,... there was this moment, and he just looked at me and..."

The phone went silent for a beat, and then Jane squealed. "He kissed you! Oh my gosh, Sarah, did he kiss you?!"

Sarah couldn't deny it anymore. "Yes!" she confessed, the word tumbling out in a rush. "It was the most perfect, magical kiss, not like the one that I froze on this morning. This one was so much more."

Jane shouted, "Wait! Two kisses. Girl, you have to tell me about the first kiss."

Sarah told Jane about the first kiss. She was a bit more embarrassed about that one. To Sarah, the kiss at the Christmas Market was her first real kiss. "Jane. And then..." She trailed off, a dreamy smile on her face. Memories of their closeness under the starlit sky, the warmth of Alex's embrace, and the unspoken promise in his eyes flooded back.

"And then?" Jane prompted, her voice filled with anticipation.

Sarah took a deep breath. "And then we just talked for hours about everything and nothing. It felt like I'd known him forever, Jane."

There was a brief silence on the other end of the line, and then a deep sigh escaped Jane's lips. "Sarah, this sounds like a Hallmark Christmas special come to life! I'm so happy for you!"

"Me too," Sarah admitted, her voice thick with emotion. "I never thought about relationships or that I'd meet someone like Alex. He's funny, kind, and..." she paused, a thoughtful note entering her voice, "surprisingly mature for a hockey player."

Jane chuckled. "Well, you can't judge a book by its cover, right? Especially not a book that looks like Alex freaking Holstead!"

Sarah sighed, a contented smile gracing her lips. "You're right. Jane, I think… I think I might be falling in love with him."

Jane's enthusiastic chatter filled the phone, showering Sarah with advice, questions, and well wishes. They chatted for a while longer, and finally, with a heavy heart, Sarah hung up.

Looking out the window, she couldn't help but look at the little snowflake ornament hanging on the windowsill. Maybe, just maybe, this holiday season wouldn't just be about her failed ice skating career and missing family and traditions. Maybe this season was about building something truly special with Alex and teaching Sarah there were things more important in life than being a champion.

CHAPTER EIGHT

NEVERMIND!

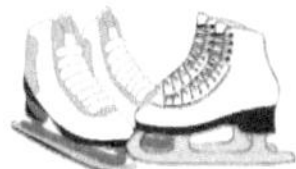

The clinking of forks against plates and the aroma of grilled meat filled the air as Alex recounted his evening with Sarah at the Christmas market. Benson leaned back in his chair, shoveling fries into his mouth with a thoughtful expression.

"It sounds like the magic of the season rubbed off on you," Benson said, taking a swig of his beer. I've never seen you so smitten."

Alex chuckled, a goofy grin plastered on his face. "Yeah, it was something special. We just clicked, you know? Like we'd known each other for ages."

He described Sarah's infectious laughter, their shared love of terrible Christmas sweaters, and the way her eyes sparkled under the twinkling lights. As he spoke, a warmth spread through his chest, a feeling he hadn't experienced before.

Benson laughed, "You are in deep. You bought matching ugly sweaters and wore them in public. I hope someone took a picture of this."

Alex rarely blushed, but the way Benson said it made him

feel embarrassed for giving into Sarah's whim, or was it his whim, and he currently wanted to blame it on her.

"So, what are you thinking for date number three?" Benson asked, snapping Alex out of his reverie.

"What do you mean, date three? That was our first date."

Benson drank his beer, rolled his eyes over the rim, and put the bottle down. "Alex, Sarah is the first girl you ever invited to sit behind the glass. In the eight years we've been friends, you have never once dated anyone long-term or thought highly of them enough to bring them to meet the team. That was date one. Date two was the Christmas Market, which was definitely more 'romantic' than dodging pucks and screaming fans?"

Alex rubbed his hand over his chin, flipping through the mental Rolodex of Halifax's typical holiday events. "Maybe… buy a tree together? There's that huge tree lot by the waterfront…"

"Cliché, but cute," Benson interrupted with a smirk. "Just don't expect her to fall for you because you can pick a tree."

With Alex's good leg, he kicked Benson under the table. "Shut up, man. I just want to spend time with her."

The playful banter took a serious turn as Alex admitted, almost in a whisper, "Benson, I think I'm falling for her. This feels different… real."

Benson raised an eyebrow, a concerned crease forming between his eyes. "Hold up. Isn't this a little too fast? You've only known this girl for a month, and her career is over. Remember, she's got a whole life back in Louisiana to go to, and she even said that was where she was going when she's done with her recovery. What happens when she wants to go back home expecting you to follow? You are still in your prime, and not to be selfish, but you can't leave the team yet. We promised to retire together, and I am not ready to end my career just because you found a sweet girl and want to do right by her."

Alex flinched, a cold dread settling in his stomach. He hadn't considered any of that. Was that what he was doing? Falling for Sarah's innocence instead of her? She was refreshing compared to the other women he's been with. Could that be all it is? Sarah had mentioned wanting to return, but he'd pushed it aside in the whirlwind of their connection. If he was really serious and falling in love with her, would he be able to give up his career at the drop of a hat if she tells him she wouldn't stay with him? Will she want marriage first, or will she forget about her conservative nature and move in with him if he says he doesn't want to leave?

"And there's the age difference," Benson continued, breaking him away from his thoughts. Benson's voice was gentle and reiterated the thought he had just had. "Fool around, sure, but are you ready for something serious? Can you imagine giving up your career here for someone you just met? None of our team is married. Even coach is single. We have long days during the season and travel a lot. WAGS don't travel with the teams, leading to a lack of trust because of all the puck bunnies that follow us around, and the divorce rate is at ninety percent. Do you want to drag a wife into that? I know Sarah is used to traveling too, being an ice princess, but what we do is different."

Alex choked out the word "Wife." Both men were silent as the questions hung heavy in the air. Alex stared down at his beer, the once-joyful memories tinged with a newfound worry. He loved hockey. It was his life. But the way Sarah made him feel – the laughter, the connection, the spark – that was something he couldn't ignore either.

"I don't know," Alex admitted, his voice laced with uncertainty. "I just know I don't want to let her go."

Benson put his hand on Alex's shoulder, his expression filled with empathy. "Remember when I met that girl Alishia, and we jumped into marriage in my mid-twenties? I am one of those statistics ready to take the plunge. Within the first six months of our relationship, once married, her trust went into the trash even though I was being faithful, and not even a year after we said I do, we were filing for divorce. All I am saying is I put a lot of thought into this. That is why I don't get serious with anyone, and I don't want you to make the same mistakes. Take it slow."

Alex nodded, a wave of gratitude washing over him. He needed this reality check. He couldn't let his newfound feelings cloud his judgment. He had a career, a life he'd built in Halifax. But Sarah… there was something undeniable about her, but he needed to get to know her better before jumping into his feelings."Love shouldn't be this complicated, right?"

"Love is messy, Alex," Benson said gently. "But it also shouldn't force you to make impossible choices. You need to talk to her to figure out where you both stand. Falling in love is easy, but building a future together… takes work, communication, and a lot of reality."

Alex stared at his untouched food. The festive cheer of the restaurant suddenly dimmed by the weight of Benson's words. He knew his friend was right. He was falling for Sarah, and it felt incredible. But before allowing himself to get swept away completely, he had some serious soul-searching to do. Could their connection survive the distance, the age difference, and the disparate paths their lives seemed destined to take? Only time and honest conversation would tell.

"Thanks," he said, a determined glint returning to his eyes. I guess I'll figure it out. One date, one conversation at a time." Alex said, and then the men both turned their attention to finishing their steak and discussing where the team was headed.

The silence from Alex stretched long into the next day. Each unanswered text notification made Sarah's stomach twist a little tighter. Had he changed his mind about her? Was the magic of the Christmas market just a fleeting moment?

The urge to text and bombard him with messages about how amazing she thought their date was, warred with her pride. She didn't want to seem desperate or clingy, especially not to a man ten years her senior. She already messed up on her first kiss and real date.

Just when she was about to resign herself to the possibility of him disappearing like a snowflake in a heatwave, his phone call rang out. Relief flooded her, followed by a nervous flutter in her chest.

"Hey Sarah," Alex's voice sounded warm despite the distance of the phone. How about an early dinner tonight? We can chat, and then there's this amazing Christmas light show at the marina I thought we could check out," he paused and said, "It starts at 8 p.m., so if you're interested, I could pick you up at six."

The disappointment she hadn't realized she was harboring melted away. "That sounds…" she started to give a generic answer, then changed to her real feelings, "I'd love to," she managed, a smile breaking out.

Dinner ended up being a tightrope walk of emotions. It started alright. They talked about their day, Sarah detailing her frustrations with therapy and being bored again now that Alex was released to start his rehab back on the ice. Alex recounted that even with his brace, being back on the ice was a bit rough. Yet, a shadow hung over their conversation.

Then, the conversation turned to Alex asking Sarah about her plans for when she was done with therapy, and that was when the cracks began to show. Sarah mentioned her plans about returning to Cypressville, maybe even returning to school. Then, when Alex responded with his intentions about playing hockey for another three years, a jolt of reality went straight through Sarah's heart. Three years. It seemed like a lifetime in the face of their budding connection. What did that mean for them? Did he expect her to move here? She didn't have the money or the work visa to do that. She was an American citizen and could only stay while on the team, and that time was nearly up. She didn't have a choice she would have to go home.

Then, as if sensing her unspoken question, Alex dropped the bomb. "This is a great holiday romance, right?"

His words felt like a bucket of ice water. The joy of their first kiss, the stolen glances at the market – all reduced to a temporary fling? Shame burned in her cheeks; she was nothing but a puck bunny to him, and she forced a smile. "Absolutely," she choked out, trying to sound casual, but she knew that she must have been turning pale at the rate her stomach sank. "A wonderful first experience. Thank you, and you've been so gentlemanly. I'm glad my first kiss was with you."

There was a beat of silence, then a strained chuckle from Alex. "It wouldn't have been the same with anyone else."

She sensed he was trying to be playful, but he failed, and the words landed with a heavy thud, making her feel even sicker. All she wanted to do was go home, but she had to play this through. She wouldn't let him see how devastated she was, so she played along.

"I doubt anyone could match up with Mr. Hockey Hottie,"

she joked, using Jane's nickname. "Definitely, I have some major bragging points when I get home," she said, echoing his sentiments. She shivered as a chill settled over her despite the warmth of the restaurant.

The rest of the evening was a blur of just trying to make it through without crying and faking her having a good time. Alex held her hand, a gesture that offered no comfort the entire night. And the light show, although a dazzling display of colors and merriment, failed to illuminate the darkness that had settled between them. Finally, the night ended. As Sarah stood at her door, the unspoken words hung heavy in the air.

"Thanks for tonight, Alex," she whispered, tears pricking her eyes. "It was… fun."

"You too, Sarah," he replied, his voice devoid of warmth.

He leaned in, kissed her cheek, turned away, and headed to his car.

The cheek kiss, a cruel reminder of the chasm between their ages and dreams, was too much to bear. Sarah forced a smile, her heart breaking with each beat as she waved goodbye. He took off down the street, tears finally spilling down her cheeks as she leaned against the door.

The harsh reality of the situation sinking in. The fairytale date only two days ago at the Christmas market had morphed into a cruel reminder of her inexperience and the vast gulf dating. All she could do now was call Jane, pour out her heart, and let the tears wash away the disappointment, hoping that amidst the wreckage, a path forward would reveal itself.

CHAPTER NINE

SAYING GOODBYE TO THE DREAM

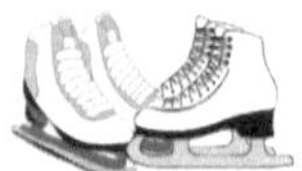

The week crawled by, and a single cryptic text exchanges with Alex marked the time that passed. Short messages danced around their unspoken feelings, leaving Sarah with a bittersweet ache. Christmas was a mere week away, and with it came her one-way ticket back to Cypressville, departing January 4th.

The looming departure cast a long shadow. Sarah had begun packing, a melancholic ritual of folding memories into massive suitcases. Her dorm life hadn't resulted in much accumulation; most of the space was swallowed by the ghosts of skating sessions past – sequined leotards, worn-out boots, and practice jerseys that whispered of victories and defeats. In the corner of her suitcase, tucked away amongst the sports attire, lay a small, glittering snowflake ornament – a silent remembrance of their first magical date. A tear escaped her eye as she picked it up, pressing it to her cheek.

"I wish we could have been a real couple," she whispered, the ornament cool against her skin. "I'm going to miss you."

Leaving was the only logical choice. The longer Sarah stayed, the deeper she fell and the harder the goodbye would be. Her visa was tied to her position on the team, and with her PT ending, her time was running out anyway. Marrying Alex for a visa flashed through her mind – a desperate, reality-TV-worthy idea quickly dismissed. She confided in Jane about it, the absurdity of the thought making them both laugh, but a flicker of longing remained beneath the humor.

At her final physical therapy session, Sarah balanced precariously on her recovering ankle, Lindsey's voice a constant presence behind her. "I'm going to miss you," her therapist said, a mischievous glint in her eyes. "Watching you and Alex get together was the highlight of my month."

Sarah gritted her teeth, forcing a smile. "Well, it was fun while it lasted."

Lindsey wouldn't let it go. "He always seemed like fun," she said, her voice dropping to a conspiratorial whisper. "Wouldn't mind a little fun myself, even if it's just one night, you know?"

Sarah knew exactly what she meant. Lindsey had been relentlessly trying to pry into Sarah's relationship with Alex.

"Hey now," boomed a voice behind them, making them both jump. Alex stood there, a playful glint in his eyes. "I don't mess around like that, Lindsey. Plus, Sarah's not that kind of girl."

Lindsey scurried away, leaving Sarah and Alex alone.

"My discharge session," Sarah explained, a blush creeping up her cheeks. "I'll be able to continue the strengthening exercises on my own."

Alex looked at her for a long moment and then surprised her. "I'm heading to the ice rink after this with Phil to get back on the ice for the first time. I was hoping you'd come with me."

Sarah stared at him, her heart skipping a beat. "Why?" she asked, her voice barely a whisper.

He hesitated, then finally spoke, his voice rough. "The

team's away for a game, and… well, I want someone there who really knows the ice. Someone who understands."

His words hung in the air, heavy with unspoken meaning. Was it just about needing someone to watch his back on the ice, or was it something more? Sarah's heart mirrored the slow pace of the treadmill. Disappointment gnawed at her. A part of her had desperately hoped to hear Alex confess his feelings, something more than just needing her "support" on the ice. They'd barely spoken all week, the silence a painful echo of their unspoken connection. Sleep offered a temporary escape, a refuge from the urge to call him and plead for more than stolen glances and fleeting moments.

"I don't know how much help I'd be," she admitted, her voice laced with a hint of resignation. "Being released from therapy doesn't mean I can just jump back on the ice. They want me to wait at least six months."

Alex surprised her with a genuine plea. "You'd be my support, Sarah. We've been physiotherapy buddies since day one, and having you there would mean the world to me."

Sarah watched him, a familiar tug warring with logic. She could practically feel him waiting with bated breath, a silent prayer hanging in the air. Then, Alex broke the dam of her resistance with a whispered, "Please."

"Alright, sure," she conceded, a flicker of hope sparking in her eyes. "I'll go."

Alex's grin stretched from ear to ear, a stark contrast to the fabricated reason he'd given Phil for being at the clinic. It was pure happenstance, a stroke of luck really. Overhearing Sarah's voice through the phone had yanked him back to reality. Lindsey's offhand comment had ignited a spark of possessiveness within him, the need to clarify their connection.

Seeing Sarah's downcast expression upon arrival had sent a pang of worry through him. He initially feared a setback in her recovery, but as he got closer and overheard Lindsey's suggestive remarks, anger flared within him. He wasn't some casual fling, and Sarah deserved better than being portrayed that way.

His parents' words echoed in his mind – "You only find your soulmate once in a lifetime." Was Sarah his soulmate? He wasn't sure, but with Sarah back in his presence, the silence of the past week felt like a lifetime. He wouldn't let her slip away without figuring this thing out. Her departure date of January 4th loomed closer to the horizon. He had a deadline and would use these few weeks to unravel his tangled emotions. Today, however, is an excuse to be near her again.

Sarah chuckled at his clumsy maneuvers on the ice with the skate helper.

"Shut it," he mumbled, a blush creeping up his neck. He had to admit the helper made his stride awkward. Slowly, a sliver of his confidence returned, and by the end of the session, the helper was discarded, and he slowly regained some of his former strength.

Phil bid them farewell, leaving Alex and Sarah alone in the quiet ice rink.

"You're getting stronger every day," Sarah observed, mirroring the compliment he'd offered her earlier.

"Same goes for you," he replied, his voice warm. "Can't wait to see you flying on the ice again."

A shadow crossed her features. "I'm not sure I ever will. Cypressville doesn't have a rink."

Alex nudged her playfully. "If there's a will, there's a way, Sarah. And I know you. You won't give it up forever. Ice is in our blood."

Sarah met his gaze, a question lingering in her eyes. Was there more to his word than the bittersweet goodbye she knew was coming? Did she want to find out?

They ended up spending the rest of the evening together. The strain was gone, and it was as if they had never stopped talking for a week. The conversation easily flowed as they ate dinner, drank wine, and shared stories about their youth, their laughter mingling with the holiday tunes playing in the background.

Despite the joy of the day spent with Alex, melancholy struck Sarah in the chest as the dinner winded down. As she tried to rub the ache away, she spoke softly, needing to get her thoughts out. "I love being here with you, and sometimes you make me not want to go home, but I miss Cypressville," she confessed. "But no matter how much I love…" she stumbled over, nearly admitting she loved him. She rubbed the ache in her chest again, "Being here with you, I know it won't last, and my grandpa is my only family, and I miss him, and if I hadn't met you, I would probably be on a plane tomorrow heading home to be with him for Christmas, and now I feel so selfish and guilty that I'm not, especially knowing what we have isn't in our stars."

Alex's gaze softened, a pang of empathy shooting through him. His heart leaped when he thought she would confess, and he was defeated when she didn't. But he also understood the pull of home, the comfort of familiar faces, especially when you've been gone a long time. He longed to tell her how much he dreaded her departure, but the words wouldn't come.

Their future remained unwritten, a painful truth shrouded in the festive spirit. As they walked to his car, they both were lost in their thoughts and when he arrived at her place, he walked her to the door. Before Sarah went in, he grabbed her hand. "I know you miss home, and I know what I'm about to ask is selfish, but I want to spend Christmas with you. I need to know what this is…" he was silent momentarily.

He leaned down, his lips mere inches from hers, and whispered, "Maybe it is in our stars." Sarah pressed her finger over his lips as he was about to kiss her. He backed away, and her eyes watered. She croaked, "Please don't." Then he whispered, "I'm scared."

Alex pulled her into an embrace, "I am too," he said, holding her to his chest and whispering in her ear, "Please, Sarah, just give me until you leave. Both of us should know by then what this is. Neither of us expected this, and the timing is crap, but don't we owe it to ourselves to discover if what this is, is real?" The last words came out in a gruff, choked tone.

CHAPTER TEN

FORGET GOODBYES, LIVE THE DREAM

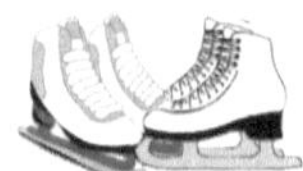

The aroma of old paper and brewing coffee filled the air as Sarah browsed the shelves. Alex hadn't left Sarah's side since the day after they went to the ice rink. He even packed a bag and stayed on her couch, wanting to spend every moment with her to figure out their feelings. As the days passed, her feelings only grew stronger and even more confused. Neither of them broached the subject of whether the relationship was the real thing or how they would make it work.

Sarah picked up a book she spotted called *Making Long Distance Work* and laid it under the romance novel she picked out for Jane. Christmas carols played softly in the background, creating a warm and inviting atmosphere, and Alex returned with a cup of hot chocolate. "Thank you," she said after she took a sip.

The warm chocolate tasted rich and creamy, "this is delicious. Did they add cinnamon?"

He nodded and then picked up a book off the shelf. Look at this *Acadian 'Cajun' folktale, a tale of two worlds.* "Do you think your Grandpa would like this?" Alex asked.

Sarah read the back of the book and couldn't believe Alex found a book here that mentioned Louisiana. It was as if it were a sign that maybe she and Alex could blend their worlds. "Yes, I think it is a perfect gift for Grandpa. His mother was from Acadiana." Alex lifted his brow in question. "That's a region in Louisiana where most of the Acadians settled when they left Canada."

A pang of homesickness hit her but didn't last long when she spotted a book on the fifty-off table, and a mischievous grin spread across her face. She picked up *The Hockey Player's Guide to Flirting Like a Gentleman* and snuck it into her basket underneath the other books. She would save it as a joke gift for Alex to tease him later if their relationship turned into something more.

Suddenly, his deep voice startled her. "What is that?"

Sarah tried shifting the basket behind her, but Alex was too quick. He peeked in the basket at the stack of romance novels. "I didn't realize you were that into romance."

She breathed a sigh of relief. "I enjoy them here or there, but everything here is a gift, so no more snooping, mister." She ended with a teasing laugh.

Alex chuckled, "One thing you need to know is that I don't read anything that isn't about hockey." His response made her laugh out loud, and then she said, "I'll remember that."

"Why is that so funny?" he asked warily.

"I can't imagine many books about hockey. Once again, you and I are alike— we both rarely read." Sarah made up on the fly.

"You got me. I am not a reader. I prefer watching TV."

"Same here."

Alex grabbed the basket, "I promise I won't look just in case there is something for me in there, and if there is, I promise to read it because you gave it to me."

Sarah smiled, "I'll keep you to that promise." Then she said, "Thanks for finding the book on Acadians. I can't wait to give it to my grandpa."

They continued browsing, picking out gifts for their families. Sarah watched Alex as he meticulously chose cookbooks for his parents, a hint of tenderness in his expression.

"You seem to know your parents well," she said softly.

Alex glanced at her, a smile gracing his lips. "They're pretty amazing. You'll have to meet them someday."

The weight of his words hung in the air. Someday. A future together, a future Sarah wasn't sure of. But seeing him talk about his family, a warmth bloomed in her chest. Maybe, just maybe, there could be more than a holiday fling. He may be starting to see something further in the future. She wouldn't bug him about what-ifs now. She wants to enjoy their time together, but by the time she leaves to return home, Sarah plans to sit down with him and have an earnest conversation about their future.

The afternoon turned into evening, and the twinkling lights of the Christmas spirit were on every street corner. The street lamps were woven with garland and wreaths, and the snow covering the ground made this Christmas postcard perfect. In the distance, Sarah could hear the bell choir performing her favorite Christmas tune, *Carol of the Bells*.

Alex was holding Sarah's gloved hand in one hand and all of her shopping bags in the other and chatting about how the weight of her gifts would help him keep his strength up for when he returned to the Hurricanes. Alex had been inserting comments daily about his return to work. She knew what it was like to live a dream, and she wasn't selfish enough to beg him to retire and move to Cypressville with her. But she did wish he would broach the topic of what they were.

She hadn't let him kiss her since they got back together. She was worried that it would make her have trouble leaving him when the time came, and each day, she tried to tell herself they were just friends. Friends could hold hands, at least right. She rationalized at least that bit of intimacy with him.

As they walked up the few steps to Sarah's apartment, she reached inside her purse for her keys when her phone rang. It was a Louisiana number, but it wasn't programmed into her phone. She turned to Alex, "Should I answer it, or do you think it's spam?"

"You should get it just in case," he advised.

"Hello?" she answered. She looked up at Alex with tears filling her eyes. Her heart plummeted as she listened to the voice on the other end. Her grandpa needed emergency surgery, a triple bypass. He asked them to call Sarah to come home, and he wouldn't consent to surgery before seeing her.

Sarah's hand shook as she hung up. Alex had taken the keys out of her hand, opened her door, dropped the bags on the floor, and instantly scooped her into a hug. Fear gripped her heart. Her voice choked with emotion. She said, "I need to go home now. My grandpa…"

Alex's face paled. "Is he…" his words trailed off.

"Not yet, but he had a heart attack and needs surgery but won't consent to it until he sees me."

He wrapped his arms around her, holding her close as she sobbed. "You go finish packing. I am going home to pack for a few weeks and will pick you up in an hour. We are going to the airport and getting you home before tomorrow. We will not let your grandpa die. I promise."

Sarah rushed to her room, and Alex ran as fast as he could to his car without irritating his knee. He called Benson in the car. "I need a favor. Can you get your friend, who has a private jet, to fly Sarah and me to Louisiana? Her grandpa had a heart attack, and I need to get her there ASAP?"

"Shit, man, sure, I'll call him and ask. Give me ten." then hung up the phone.

Alex rushed into his place, pulled his duffle out, threw some clothes in his toiletries, and was out of his house and back on the road to Sarah's in less than twenty minutes. By the time he arrived, Sarah had packed her suitcases and was on the phone with the landlord. "...I won't be back. Thank you." she hung up the phone.

Alex took one of her suitcases. She placed the key on the tray by the door, locked it, and took her other suitcase. Alex put her luggage in the trunk. Sarah was already in the front seat. She was shaking like crazy. He buckled himself in, started the car, and placed his hand over hers on her lap. "Benson got us a ride to Louisiana. We will be there in a few hours."

Sarah melted back in the seat. "Thank you." She breathed out as if it were a prayer.

CHAPTER ELEVEN

CHRISTMAS IN CYPRESSVILLE

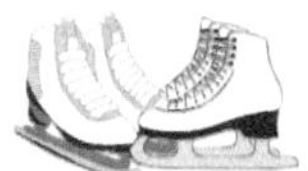

*D*ecember 23rd arrived, a stark contrast to the festive cheer Sarah had envisioned. The rented car hummed along the highway, the cityscape of Alexandria looming ahead. Her heart pounded a frantic rhythm against her ribs, as they drove the rented car from the airport to the Alexandria hospital where her Grandpa lay.

At the hospital, Sarah rushed to her grandpa's side, the sterile white of the room felt suffocating as Sarah gripped her grandpa's frail hand. The man who once seemed larger than life now looked impossibly small, vulnerability etched on his weathered face. His once-booming voice was raspy, his usual twinkle dimmed. Holding his hand, Sarah felt a pang of guilt for not noticing the subtle signs of his illness – the shortness of breath she'd dismissed as altitude sickness.

"Sugar, I'm sorry that I'm ruining your Christmas," he rasped, his voice barely above a whisper.

Sarah forced a smile, her voice thick with emotion. "You aren't ruining anything. We'll celebrate Christmas once you're back on your feet, stronger than ever."

Her Grandpa coughed weakly, his gaze drifting to Alex,

who stood solemnly by the doorway. "If I don't make it, I want you to know that I like that young man who brought you to me. He's one of a kind, Sarah. Don't miss the opportunity to see where it leads. I'm grateful every day your grandma took a chance on me, leaving the city life to live with a country boy. Before your momma and you, she was the only woman on earth worth loving."

A fresh wave of tears welled up in Sarah's eyes. Memories of her parents, lost in a car accident when she was just a child, flooded back. Her grandparents had been her rock, her anchor. It was her Grandma who had introduced her to the magic of ice skating, but her Grandpa, with his unwavering support and countless drives to distant rinks, had been her biggest cheerleader.

Swallowing back a sob, Sarah squeezed his hand. "Don't talk like that. You'll be in recovery soon, telling bad jokes and making me eat more of Grandma's pecan pie than I should."

A flicker of his old spirit returned to his eyes. "Maybe I will, Sugar. But remember what I said." His voice grew fainter as they prepped him for surgery. "Those feelings you have for Alex, they're real. Don't let fear hold you back. Talk him into opening an ice rink here; if he loves you, he'll follow you home. I love you, Sugar."

Those were the last coherent words Sarah heard as the medical staff wheeled her Grandpa away. Tears streamed down her face as she turned to Alex, his own eyes filled with concern. He opened his arms, and Sarah collapsed into his embrace, grief and fear momentarily eclipsed by the warmth of his presence.

"He better not die," she choked out, clinging to him. "He's all the family I have left.."

Alex held her tight, his heart aching for her. He had never been in the situation where someone he cherished was ill or could potentially pass away. He didn't have the answers, but he could offer comfort, a shoulder to cry on, and a fierce hope that her Grandpa would pull through.

Seeing her pain awakened a fierce protectiveness within him. He was grateful, for the first time since his injury, that hockey would have to wait. It gave him the opportunity to be here for her, to offer comfort and a listening ear in her time of need. They could navigate their feelings later, explore the uncharted territory of their connection. For now, their focus was singular: her grandfather's health.

As Sarah pulled back, wiping a tear from her cheek, Alex squeezed her hand gently. "Don't be sorry," he murmured, his voice thick with concern. "A sweater can dry. You, on the other hand, need all your strength." He gestured towards the cafeteria. "Let's grab some coffee. You must be exhausted."

The small, brightly lit cafeteria, festive decorations adorning the sterile walls, offered a welcome refuge from the sterile hospital environment. Sarah pointed out familiar faces – Jane, her ever-supportive friend, and Walter, her grandfather's loyal companion from Cypressville. There was also Jane's Aunt Matilda, a kind-faced woman with a knowing smile.

Jane wasted no time, rushing over and engulfing Sarah in a hug. "How is he? How are you holding up?" Her voice was a torrent of worry, reflecting the love they shared for Sarah's grandfather.

Sarah took a shaky breath, stealing a glance at Alex for silent support. "They're taking him into surgery now," she finally managed, her voice choking with emotion. "The doctor said... said it's a triple bypass."

A collective gasp echoed through the small group, the weight of the situation settling upon them like a heavy cloak.

The festive cheer that had adorned their thoughts just moments ago vanished, replaced by the stark reality of the situation. Yet, amidst the fear and uncertainty, a flicker of hope remained. They were a small circle, bound by love and a fierce determination to support Sarah during this ordeal.

Aunt Matilda, a woman whose life experience seemed etched in the lines around her eyes, sprung into action. Digging through her purse, she retrieved an ancient cell phone and a worn address book. Her reading glasses, secured by a string around her neck, perched precariously on her nose as she dialed a number. "We need a prayer chain," she announced to the room, her voice resolute despite the tremor in her hands.

Walter, Sarah's grandfather's friend, extended a calloused hand towards Alex. "Walter Rabalais," he introduced himself with a warm smile, "I own Main Street Java back in Cypressville. George and I go way back." He paused, his gaze flickering between Alex and Sarah. "He didn't mention Sarah having a significant other."

Caught off guard by the personal question, Alex fumbled for a response. Walter, sensing his discomfort, chuckled good-naturedly. "Don't mind me, son. Down here in the South, we're a touch nosy and friendly. We know everyone's business, and no stranger ever goes unnoticed."

Shaking Walter's hand, Alex offered his own name, carefully avoiding any mention of his relationship with Sarah. The truth was, he wasn't entirely sure what it was himself.

"Son," he began, his voice dropping to a low murmur, "let me give you a piece of advice, two actually. First, one bite of our Southern cooking, and you'll never want to leave. Second, that girl," he gestured towards Sarah, "she's the apple of George's eye. If you're serious about her, talk to him when he's on the mend. George, that man's a walking encyclopedia of love. He and Gertrude, they were married for fifty years -

married at sixteen, mind you, which wasn't exactly the norm back then. But they knew, son, they just knew. And according to George, 'when you know, you know.'" Walter's eyes clouded over with a hint of sadness he patted Alex's shoulder. "Can't say I disagree," he said as he headed back to the table.

Walter's unsolicited advice hung in the air, as Alex watched Sarah, a picture of quiet concern. She was an incredible woman, there she sat although fear for her grand-pa's wellbeing showed in her body language she still listened patiently as Jane's voice filled the air. He headed back to the table and sat beside Sarah, her ice cold hand reached for his. He scooted closer and grabbed both her hands into his as she and Jane discussed Christmas.

"Oh, I know!" Jane said, full steam, "So as not to over-whelm George while in the hospital for recovery. Why don't we do twelve days of Christmas for him?"

Alex noticed a hint of interest break through Sarah's solum expressions and chimed in. "What a great idea. Maybe I can learn about Cypressville at the same time as finding local gifts to fit the song and bring him small tokens to match the song."

Jane was quick to catch on. "Yes, like for two turtle doves, we can bring him some homemade turtles made out of dove chocolate."

Sarah had a hit of a smile appear. "You know grandpa loves his sweets, maybe we can buy a twelve-pack of drum-stick ice creams for drummers drumming?"

Walter chimed in, "Or his favorite fried chicken drum-sticks, by the twelfth day I'm sure he will be starving for some real food instead of this hospital mash."

Matilda laughed "This will be fun. I can make him donuts for five golden rings and dust them with edible gold dust and sugar."

The lighthearted talk helped lift the heavy atmosphere. Alex watched Sarah, his heart swelling with a tenderness he couldn't quite explain. Sitting in a hospital cafeteria, in a small southern town wasn't what he ever envisioned in his future, nor the ache and longing to be next to someone that he was beginning to — he stopped his thoughts. Too much was hanging over their head to think about that right now. For now he'd just be here, and present for Sarah so that she knew she wasn't alone. Sarah finally met his gaze, a silent understanding passed between them. Her hands warmed by his, she squeezed them, that small gesture told him all he needed. They would face this together, one uncertain step at a time.

CHAPTER TWELVE

I'M NOT SCROOGE

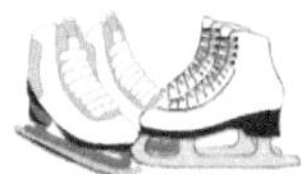

The Louisiana humidity hung heavy in the air, a stark contrast to the crisp Canadian winters Alex was accustomed to. Christmas with no snow, pushing eighty degrees, was a completely new experience. Sarah remained at the hospital overnight, keeping vigil by her Grandpa's bedside in the ICU. Matilda, with her characteristic Southern hospitality, had offered Alex a place to stay and celebrate Christmas Eve together.

Morning arrived with a glimmer of hope. News broke that George was awake, albeit cranky – a development Walter considered a positive sign. Alex managed a few phone calls with Sarah, his heart heavy with her worry. She described her Grandpa as pale and frail, her voice thick with emotion. During one such speakerphone conversation, as Alex fumbled with the coffee pot, Matilda entered the room, her walker clicking rhythmically on the hardwood floor.

"What do you expect, sugar?" she quipped, catching the tail end of Sarah's words. "Your Grandpa's pushing eighty. He's bound to look a little frail at this point."

Matilda poured herself a cup of coffee, placing it on the

walker's tray before returning to the living area. Sarah, choking back a sob, whispered into the phone, "I wish you were here. Being alone with him is so hard, Alex. It's depressing. I just wish I could take away his pain."

At a loss for words, Alex offered the only comfort he could. "Did the doctors say how long he'd be in the ICU?"

"They said all his vitals are good," Sarah replied. "If all stays well overnight, they think he may move into a regular room sometime tomorrow."

An idea sparked in Alex's mind. "Would you like me to go to the hospital tomorrow? I could hang out in the waiting room, just be there. And if they move your Grandpa to a private room, maybe we can surprise him with our first-day-of-Christmas gift for him."

A sniffle escaped Sarah. "But it's Christmas," she protested. "Don't you want to be somewhere besides a hospital all day?"

His heart ached for her. "Sarah," he began, then stopped. The words "I love you" threatened to tumble out, but he choked them back, his pulse hammering in his chest.

"Alex?" Sarah's voice crackled with concern. "Hello? Are you there?"

He cleared his throat, his voice rough. "Yeah, sorry. I just... I want to be with you. I don't mind waiting all day, not if it means being there for you."

A soft sob reached him through the phone. "I want to be with you too," she confessed. "Thank you, Alex. Thank you for being here through all this. I don't know what I would've done without you."

"You would have been fine," he countered gently. "You're a strong, independent woman who can handle anything. You would have found a way, relied on this amazing support system you have here in Cypressville. Honestly, I can't remember the last time I felt so welcome in a new place, surrounded by strangers who instantly felt like family."

A watery chuckle escaped Sarah. "I'm glad Jane and everyone else are taking good care of you."

Seemingly to lighten the mood, Alex changed the subject. "Speaking of family, a few more townspeople are dropping by for Christmas Eve dinner. Maybe that's the perfect opportunity to brainstorm some ideas for your Grandpa's first-day-of-Christmas gift."

Hope flickered in Sarah's voice. "That's a good idea, Alex. Thank you."

The conversation continued, a tentative bridge built across the miles separating them. As they hung up, Alex leaned against the counter, a newfound sense of purpose settling over him. He was here for Sarah, for however long fate allowed. And together, they would face whatever challenges this Christmas, and the uncertain future, held.

The warmth of the Christmas Eve dinner spread through Alex, a stark contrast to the chill of isolation he'd expected. Nestled around the expansive dining table, a festive scene straight out of a Norman Rockwell painting, Alex felt a surprising sense of belonging. Each plate, adorned with gold rims and a different whimsical Christmas scene, gleamed under the soft glow of the chandelier.

Six figures filled the chairs: Jane, Matilda, and Walter, familiar faces by now. Two new men joined the mix – Mr. Stevens, an elderly gentleman with a twinkle in his eye, and Frank, a man in his fifties recently widowed, facing a lonely Christmas without his daughter, an event planner trapped by the demands of her job. Across from Alex sat another newcomer, a single woman perhaps a decade his senior, whose fiery spirit crackled as she discussed revitalizing Main Street and Marshall Street, the corner that she believed should be buzzing with life just outside Matilda's window.

The way she spoke was charismatic and had even him a perfect stranger envisioning Cypressville as an up and coming boutique town. Apparently, her attempt to enlist the help of the current mayor, Mr. Chauvin, had been met with a resounding slam of the door. All Alex knew was that if he lived there he would vote for Andrea.

Alex's gaze swept across the table, taking in the animated faces bathed in the warm glow of the Christmas lights. The air buzzed with the continued cacophony of chatter, punctuated by bursts of infectious laughter here and there. An unfamiliar feeling bloomed in his chest – a sense of belonging. Here, amidst this boisterous gathering of strangers-turned-family, Alex felt a connection he hadn't anticipated. This wasn't the Christmas he'd envisioned, far from the quiet solitude he expected. Yet, there was a warmth, a genuineness in this makeshift family that resonated deep within him.

This wasn't the Christmas he'd envisioned, away from his family and facing an uncertain future with Sarah. Yet, an undeniable truth settled in his gut – this boisterous, open-hearted community felt more like home than he'd ever realized. These people were so unlike his own reserved family. They wore their hearts on their sleeves. They were open, friendly, and accepted you as if you were family, and that feeling drew him in like a crackling fireplace on a snowy night. Alex had never encountered such genuine warmth, such a willingness to embrace new faces, and for the first time, the isolation of his own life flickered into stark contrast. Here, in Cypressville, connection was as natural as breathing, a comforting balm to the anxieties gnawing at him.

As spoons clinked against dessert plates and the aroma of coffee swirled in the air, Jane reignited the discussion of their twelve-day Christmas plan for George. The newcomers eagerly tossed in ideas, their enthusiasm as boundless as the

Christmas spirit itself. Alex, with a phone balanced precariously between his ear and shoulder, relayed Sarah's suggestions into the mix. A flurry of activity ensued. Mr. Stevens, with a mischievous glint in his eye, volunteered to draw a partridge to be tied to a pear with a festive green ribbon – the first of their twelve gifts. Laughter filled the room as they debated the finer points of each day's offerings – turtle candies, glazed donuts, and whimsical drumstick ice cream cones crafted to resemble the twelfth day's "drummers drumming."

By the time they finished brainstorming, the clock near midnight, the last of the guests ambled out, leaving behind a warm afterglow. As the guests departed, their goodbyes tinged with the promise of Christmas cheer to come, Matilda took Alex aside. Her eyes twinkled, and she smelled of eggnog, and grinned with amusement. She reached out, gently tugging on his tie, and as he leaned down, she patted his cheek. "You're a good boy, Alex," she declared, her voice laced with warmth. "Sarah done good picking you as her Christmas gift this year."

Alex felt a blush creep up his neck. Matilda, with her endearingly blunt demeanor, had a way of disarming him. As she shuffled down the hall, her voice reached him faintly, "Christmas miracles are in the making, Charles. Love is in the air."

Confused, Alex turned to Jane. "Who's Charles?"

A knowing smile played on Jane's lips. "That, dear Alex, was Matilda's one true love. A tragic boating accident stole him away before they could say 'I do.' Though she never loved another, her heart overflows with love for those around her. She takes in strays like us, and we all become part of her family." A chuckle escaped Jane's lips. "Well, technically, I am family. Her favorite great-niece, after all." Her voice trailed off momentarily, then picked up again as if struck by a sudden memory. "Oh, right! Matilda talks to Charles all the time. Says his spirit never left her. And honestly, the way she talks to him, you'd swear he was right here in the room."

A shiver danced down Alex's spine. "Do you think there are really ghosts here?"

Jane burst out laughing. "Bless your heart," when she realized he wasn't laughing her smile stayed wide but she did try to be encouraging. "Don't be silly, Alex! Ghosts are just stories. Nothing weird or spooky has ever happened here. Unless you're Mr Scrooge."

Despite Jane's reassurances, a seed of unease lingered in Alex's mind. He wasn't necessarily miserly with his money but lately he was feeling that way over his time. He wasn't ready to give up his career for a woman he just met no matter how much his heart was telling him he was falling in love with her. As he retreated to his room Jane called out from her doorway.

"Hey, Alex."

He poked his head out. "Yeah?"

A knowing glint shone in her eyes. "Matilda might be onto something, you know. You truly are Sarah's Christmas miracle."

A warmth bloomed in Alex's chest. Alex stammered out a response then walked into his room. He couldn't quite voice his agreement with Jane's statement, but one thing was certain he yearned to be by Sarah's side as early as possible. He wanted to bring her some fresh clothes and a small, personal gift he bought at a monogram shop downtown. The young woman inside recommended a silky sachet embroidered with Sarah's initials, and imbued with the scents that reminded him of her. A small gesture, but hopefully enough to bring a smile to her face amidst the worry.

CHAPTER THIRTEEN

PARTRIDGE FAMILY?

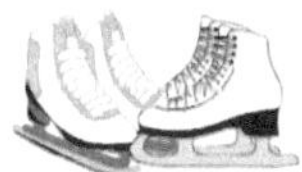

The relentless beeping of the machines was a constant counterpoint to the quiet storm within Sarah. Despite the sterile surroundings, a sliver of cautious optimism peeked through. Her grandpa, the ever-strong heart of their family, was defying her expectations. The pain was his most vocal enemy, but he battled it with the stoicism of a seasoned warrior, following doctor's orders to the letter. He'd even managed a few shaky steps with the help of a kind nurse – a feat that bordered on miraculous considering it wasn't even two full days since his open-heart surgery. Logic told her early mobilization was crucial, but in her mind, the procedures she'd endured paled in comparison to this intricate repair of the most vital organ.

Christmas morning dawned, bringing with it a flicker of excitement. A hot shower and a change of clothes beckoned, a small act of normalcy amidst the whirlwind. But the true source of her anticipation was Alex's arrival. Today, they'd have a private room, a haven where they could celebrate a makeshift Christmas and kick off the twelve-day plan. He'd be the only visitor allowed, entrusted with the whimsical drawing Mr. Stevens had created – a partridge perched proudly on a pear tree, the first symbol of their unconventional holiday cheer.

A gentle squeeze on her hand startled Sarah from her thoughts. Her grandpa's eyelids fluttered open, revealing a hint of grogginess. "Good mornin'," he rasped, his voice weak but determined.

Sarah's heart swelled with fierce joy. "Merry Christmas, Grandpa!" she exclaimed, a wide smile stretching across her face.

As if on cue, the nurse entered the room, a cart loaded with fluids and medications trailing behind her. "Merry Christmas to you too, Mr. Holstead! You did fantastic overnight. We're moving you to your own room – one step closer to going home! Transport should be up in an hour to take you down."

George's eyes lit up. "Wonderful news! Does that mean I get some real food today?"

The nurse, a woman with a twinkle in her eye, playfully pursed her lips. "Well, Mr. Holstead, Santa doesn't seem to think you've been a perfect patient this year." She feigned seriousness, glancing at her chart as if it were a naughty-or-nice list. "Looks like you teeter between the naughty and nice lists, so Santa's decided just liquids today as a compromise."

Sarah couldn't help but grin. Her grandpa's booming laugh, though laced with a hint of pain, filled the room. She quickly jumped up and grabbed a pillow, placing it strategically over his chest to offer support if his laughter intensified. The sound, a melody she hadn't heard in what felt like forever, washed over her, warming her from the inside out. It was a Christmas miracle, a testament to his fighting spirit, and the sweetest gift she could ask for.

A chirp from her phone announced a message. Alex had arrived and was waiting downstairs. The news brought a wide grin to Sarah's face, so wide her grandpa couldn't help but notice.

"Looks like that was a message from Alex," he remarked with a sly smile.

Sarah, cheeks warming slightly, offered a confirming nod.

Her grandpa, ever the observant one, continued, "I like that boy's initiative. Finding a way to get down here so quickly speaks volumes. Plus, if you two end up tying the knot, you wouldn't have to change your name. That, in my book, is a definite perk."

Sarah, mortified by the sudden turn in conversation, sputtered out a playful, "Grandpa!"

"Now, don't get flustered," he chuckled. "I'm just saying, there's a spark there, plain as day. Like when I met your grandma, or your mom met your dad. It's fate, I tell you, and fate seems to have a soft spot for our family."

Sarah rolled her eyes, though a small part of her acknowledged his words. Her parents, a testament to enduring love, had been tragically taken together. And Grandpa, despite the heartbreak of losing her grandmother, had poured that love into her, raising her with unwavering support.

"Maybe," she conceded, a hesitant note in her voice. "But things are complicated now. I'm retired, he's not. My visa expired... a long-distance relationship seems impossible. And I can't expect him to just uproot his life for me."

Her grandpa squeezed her hand gently. "Child," he said softly, "I'm not telling you what to do. I just know what I see. That boy cares for you deeply, and if it's meant to be, distance won't stand in the way. Fate has a funny way of working things out, in its own perfect timing. Just have faith."

Sarah blew a raspberry, a nervous giggle escaping her lips. Grandpa's words, though sweet, stirred up a whirlwind of emotions. Should she allow herself to hope?

He chuckled, clutching the pillow to his stomach. "Alright, alright," he wheezed. "Enough talk. Go see Alex. I'm in good hands here with the nurse. Take a break, honey. You deserve it."

"Are you sure?" she asked, her voice laced with concern.

He winked again, his mischievous grin returning. "I have my own personal nurse, don't I? Go on, shoo! I'll be fine."

Sarah leaned down and planted a kiss on his cheek. "Alright, alright," she conceded. "I'll be back soon. Love you."

With a final squeeze of his hand, she hurried out of the room, her grandpa's words echoing in her mind. Hope, a fragile bud, began to bloom in her heart. Could fate truly be on their side? With a nervous flutter in her stomach, she made her way downstairs, eager to see Alex, the uncertainty of the future momentarily eclipsed by the warmth of his presence.

Alex cut a dashing figure in the lounge, a stark contrast to his usual attire. He traded his casual clothes for slacks, a crisp dress shirt, and a tie adorned with a festive Christmas wreath. His hair, typically tousled, was tamed with a touch of gel, revealing the sharp angles of his face and the warmth of his eyes. Even his beard seemed to be neatly trimmed, an unspoken effort for this unexpected visit.

Sarah's breath hitched. Here he was, in her hometown, a thousand miles from his own life, all to be with her and her family. A warmth bloomed in her chest, a feeling more intense than anything she'd ever known. It was love, pure and unadulterated, washing over her like a tidal wave.

Before she could stop herself, she rushed into his arms, burying her face in his chest. Tears, of relief and gratitude, streamed down her cheeks, wetting the fabric of his shirt.

Alex, his face etched with concern, fumbled with the small tote bag he was carrying before dropping it to the floor, and wrapped his arms around her tightly. He enveloped her in a tight embrace, his hold both gentle and reassuring. Pulling back slightly, he cupped her face in his hands, his gaze searching hers. "What's wrong? Did something happen to your grandpa?" The worry in his voice, laced with a tenderness that sent shivers down her spine, only intensified her tears.

Shaking her head rapidly, she choked out, "N-no, it's not Grandpa. I'm just... I'm so happy to see you. All these emotions just came flooding in, and..."

The sentence remained unfinished as Alex, with a tenderness that took her breath away, pulled her back into his embrace. This time, he nestled his head in hers, his lips brushing softly against the crown of her head.

"I missed you too," he murmured, his voice barely a whisper. The words, infused with a raw vulnerability, sent a shiver down her spine. Had she imagined it, or was there a deeper meaning veiled in his quiet words? The uncertainty was both exhilarating and terrifying. Yet, as she held him close, a fragile hope flickered to life within her. Perhaps, grandpa was right, fate would make it work.

Their conversation flowed for over an hour, a gentle ebb and flow that touched upon everything and nothing. Alex's hand remained a comforting presence in hers, a silent promise of support.

"Before we head up," he said finally, reaching for the tote bag. "This is for you – a change of clothes and some essentials Jane helped put together. I wish I could've brought them yesterday."

Sarah accepted the bag with a grateful smile. "Thank you, Alex. It's perfect. Don't worry, I have a few things in my purse." She gave the bag a cursory shake. "Though, I do feel bad pawning you off on our friends and abandoning you. Pineville's a bit of a drive from here, especially considering you're unfamiliar with the area. I shouldn't have hesitated to mention it, but if you'd rather go back..."

Alex cut her off gently, placing a finger over her lips. "My holiday leave lasts until January 8th, and I plan on spending it right here. Don't you try to get rid of me so easily," he teased with a smile. "Besides, I'm invested now – gotta see these twelve days of Christmas through, wouldn't you agree?"

Sarah couldn't help but smile. "I can't wait to see Grandpa's reaction," she admitted, a mischievous glint in her eyes. "I'm almost tempted to keep him in the dark and see if he catches on."

Alex clapped his hands together with childlike enthusiasm. "That's perfect! It'll add to the surprise."

The playful mood was shattered by the sudden shrill of Sarah's phone. With a frown etched on her face, she answered the call. After a brief conversation with the nurse, Sarah hung up, her brow furrowed.

Alex's gaze held concern. "Room already?"

"Not exactly," Sarah said, her voice laced with disappointment. "When he laughed this morning, it... well, it affected his breathing. He's on oxygen now, and the doctor wants him to stay in ICU for another night."

"Oh, Sarah, I'm so sorry," Alex said, his voice warm with empathy. "You go be with him. You should be right by his side. I can leave."

Sarah shook her head. "No, the doctor said you can come up for twenty minutes, since it's Christmas. But honestly I'm bummed I can't spend more time with you."

"Hey," Alex said gently, taking her hand. "Let's go see your grandpa. We can worry about the rest of the day later. Right now, he needs you, and you need him."

With a shared nod, they headed back upstairs. As the elevator doors closed, Sarah, overwhelmed by a sudden surge of gratitude, surprised herself. On a whim, she turned to Alex, her hands reaching for his shoulders. Standing on her tiptoes, she brought his face down to hers and planted a kiss on his lips.

It wasn't a hesitant peck, but a kiss filled with emotion – a silent expression of everything she couldn't put into words. Alex didn't hesitate. The tote bag hit the floor with a soft thud as he met her kiss wholeheartedly, his own emotions mirrored in the intensity of his response.

The elevator doors chimed, pulling Sarah and Alex back to reality. The lingering heat of their stolen kiss hung in the air, unspoken yet deeply felt.

Inside the ICU, George lay quietly, his eyes turning towards them as they entered.

"Don't fret, my Sarah girl," he rasped, a hint of concern flickering in his gaze. "I see the worry in your eyes. It's just a little fluid, post-surgery. Happens all the time." He attempted a cough, but it was cut short by a sharp wheeze.

Just then, the nurse bustled in. "Mr. Holstead, you need to let that cough out," she instructed, guiding him to clutch a pillow close to his chest. After a few ragged coughs and deep breaths, the nurse left to check his vitals.

George's gaze landed on Alex. "Merry Christmas, son," he croaked.

"Merry Christmas to you too, Mr. Holstead." Alex retrieved the drawing from his bag. "This is for you, from Mr. Stevens." He unfurled the whimsical artwork, holding it up for George's inspection.

A bewildered expression washed over George's face. He glanced at Sarah, then back at the drawing. "Uh, I think that old coot's lost his marbles," he mumbled. "Why'd he give me a picture of a bird in a tree?"

Sarah stifled a giggle, desperately trying to maintain the secrecy of the twelve days of Christmas plan. "Let me see," she chirped, winking at Alex. He grinned and passed her the drawing.

"Hmm, it's a lovely drawing though, Grandpa," she mused, holding it up. "Maybe we can frame it?"

George waved a dismissive hand. "You can have it, I won't tell. You know I'm no artist."

Sarah held the drawing closer. "But Grandpa, look how beautiful it is! I swear it almost reminds me of... a partridge. Wasn't that the bird from that TV show you liked in the seventies, the one you always told me about? Do you think Mr. Stevens was trying to remind you of the yonder years and got a little confused?"

A slow smile spread across George's face. He lifted his hand and held the drawing close, peering at it over his chest. "Dementia more like it," he chuckled weakly. "But you're right, it is a partridge. And he did color it white and yellow, just like the logo. Though they were in a van, not a tree."

Alex fought back a laugh, biting his lip. "Well, it's the thought that counts, and it definitely reflects the season."

"In that case, maybe the nurse can tape it to the wall for me. It is a nice gift, even if a little...out there." George's voice hitched slightly. "I'm sorry I ruined your Christmas," he said, his gaze flitting between Sarah and Alex.

In perfect unison, both Sarah and Alex responded, "You didn't." They looked at each other for a brief moment, a silent conversation passing between them before they chimed in again, "I wouldn't want to be anywhere else."

A genuine laugh, laced with a touch of fatigue, escaped George's lips. "Fate," he rasped, then choked back another cough.

The nurse re-entered the room, her voice gentle as she ushered Alex towards the door. "Visiting hours are almost over, dear. Mr. Holstead needs his rest."

Sarah walked over to Alex by the door and squeezed his

hand and reluctantly watched as Alex departed but he stopped and turned around. "I will be downstairs reading. I will be here until around six pm. When you find time or need a break you can come meet me in the lobby even if it's for only a few minutes."

She nodded, once more the emotions of love she wanted to express to him overflowing. She wiped the tears from her eyes before going back to her grandpa.

CHAPTER FOURTEEN

LORD A WEEPING

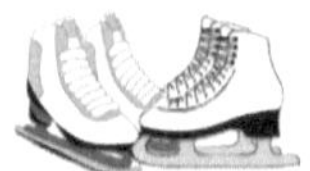

The past week had been a whirlwind for Sarah—a rollercoaster of emotions culminating in this, the tenth day of Christmas. Relief washed over her as her grandpa, finally recovered enough for discharge, caught on to the secret theme of their elaborate holiday surprise.

"Grandpa, are you happy about finally going home?" she asked, squeezing his hand gently.

"You bet I am!" he boomed, his voice regaining its usual strength. "Though, you have to admit, you made this whole hospital ordeal a lot more bearable. But speaking of bearable," he added with a mischievous glint, "I have to confess, it took me until Andrea and her choir buddies showed up with their beaks and boas to figure out what you were all up to."

Sarah couldn't help but chuckle. "They were a bit...enthusiastic, weren't they?" she admitted. "Definitely gave the game away."

George chuckled, shaking his head. "Paper cups for beaks? Honestly, the woman's got spirit. Though," he added with a playful jab, "don't go telling me I'm getting old just yet."

"Of course not," Sarah reassured him, a smile playing on her lips. "You're as sharp as ever."

"Speaking of which," Sarah interjected, her curiosity piqued, "what do you think day ten will be?"

She had only been privy to a few of the surprises, wanting to be genuinely surprised for the others. She'd made sure Alex, who was in on the whole plan, kept mum about the upcoming days.

George chuckled, his eyes twinkling with amusement. "Well, I certainly hope today's surprise involves another delicious food item. The past few days have been a culinary delight, let me tell you." He began playfully ticking off his gifts so far on his fingers.

"Walter's gumbo for one," he declared, "the first decent meal I've had since surgery. You have to get that recipe from him, Sarah. Man, that was good."

"I tried," Sarah admitted. "But he's being awfully secretive about his special ingredient."

George snorted. "Shortcut, most likely. Probably used a store-bought roux and is too embarrassed to admit it." He winked at her. "Still, the man can cook. Tell him he should take his talents to Main Street Java. They could use a good gumbo on the menu. I bet he'd bring in a crowd."

"Probably would," Sarah agreed, her phone chiming melodically. "Looks like we have visitors," she announced, checking the screen. "And it seems Walter himself will be the one giving us a ride home. Perfect timing, wouldn't you say?"

A wide grin spread across George's face. "Praise be," he muttered, relief lacing his voice. "Well, in that case, I think I'll finish getting dressed. Wouldn't want to keep Walter waiting, now would we?"

The weight of the past week seemed to lift from Sarah's shoulders as she watched her grandpa. The playful glint back in his eyes, the excitement for the unknown surprise that awaited them – it was a testament to his resilience, a victory lap after his health scare. As they embarked on the final leg of their journey home, Sarah couldn't help but feel a surge of warmth and gratitude. The twelve days of Christmas, a plan hatched in love and worry, had become more than a quirky celebration. It was a symbol of hope, a reminder of the unwavering love that surrounded them, and the joy of having her grandpa back home, healthy and whole.

The arrival of Walter and Alex brought a flurry of activity to the sterile hospital room. Sarah, overcome with relief and gratitude, threw her arms around Alex in a long hug, a blush creeping up her cheeks. She followed it up with a quick, grateful hug for Walter.

"Thank you both so much for being here," she said, her voice thick with emotion. "And thank you, Walter, for offering to take us home. Will Grandpa be getting his gift for today here, or will it wait until we get home?"

Walter and Alex exchanged a secretive glance before answering in unison, "Home."

"Oh, you two are definitely up to something!" Sarah exclaimed, a playful glint in her eyes. "He was hoping for another food gift, though."

Alex shrugged playfully, his lips curving into a grin. "I guess you'll both just have to wait and see," he teased.

Just then, George emerged from the restroom, freshly dressed and sporting a cleanly shaved face. As if on cue, the nurse bustled in, brandishing the discharge papers with a flourish. "Looks like our patient is ready to go home!" she declared.

Sarah rushed to her grandpa's side, concern flickering in her eyes as he wobbled slightly on his feet. "Whoa, slow down," she cautioned, gently guiding him back to the bed.

George swatted her hand away playfully. "I'm alright, just a little winded," he mumbled.

The nurse gave them a quick rundown of post-surgery instructions, her voice calm and reassuring. Before they knew it, Sarah and George were settled in the back seat of the car, and Alex and Walter engaged in a lively conversation in the front. Despite their short acquaintance, they seemed to have found common ground, their laughter echoing through the vehicle.

Leaning back in her seat, Sarah let a contented sigh escape her lips. Life, despite the recent scare, was unfolding in a beautiful way. She stole a glance at Alex, his profile bathed in the warm glow of the setting sun. A future with him seemed a delicious possibility, filled with stolen moments and shared dreams. The long-distance might pose a challenge, but she was a fighter. She could visit him for extended periods once her grandpa recovered further. Phone calls, video chats, quick getaways during his off-seasons – she could make it work—a couple of years, she thought, a silent promise forming in her heart. And then, when retirement beckoned for him, maybe, just maybe, he would choose to be here, with her and her grandpa. The thought ignited a spark of joy within her. Home, she realized, wasn't just a place; it was a feeling of belonging, of being surrounded by love. After the scare her grandpa had faced, she knew she could never leave again. Home was exactly where she needed to be.

Twenty minutes later, Holstead Farms came into view. A giant, hand-crafted sign stretched across the driveway, proclaiming, "Welcome Home, George!" The yard was a dazzling display of nine prancing, or perhaps leaping, Christmas reindeer.

"Seems like someone miscounted," George quipped with a smile.

Walter chuckled, a low rumble in his chest. "Maybe we did," he admitted sheepishly.

George's gaze settled on a reindeer that looked more like a melted candle than a majestic stag. "Where'd you unearth those old things?" he inquired, amusement lacing his voice.

"Dug them out of the storage unit behind my cafe," Walter explained. "Alex helped string new lights and, well, reshape them a bit."

George chuckled, shaking his head. "Here I was, thinking y'all were bringing me some frog legs for dinner."

Walter grinned. "Sorry to disappoint, but food's not on the menu today."

"Oh no," George groaned dramatically. "Sarah, we shouldn't have declined that hospital dinner! Now you'll be stuck grocery shopping, and neither of us has been here in days."

"Don't worry about that, Grandpa," Sarah reassured him, stealing a glance at Alex. His eyes twinkled with a secret amusement that sent a thrill through her. Maybe the surprise wasn't over yet.

They continued up the long driveway, and Sarah spotted Jane's car parked alongside several unfamiliar vehicles.

"What's all this about?" George boomed, curiosity piqued.

Alex, ever the gentleman, hopped out first and opened the car door for George. "Welcome home party," he announced with a flourish.

As Sarah emerged from the car, she caught a glimpse of a tear glistening on her grandpa's cheek. She squeezed his hand gently. "Grandpa, you're one lucky man," she said softly. "You have some amazing friends."

Leaning heavily on Sarah, George shuffled toward the house, a chorus of warm greetings erupting from the assembled crowd. "Welcome home, George!" they cheered.

"You're right, Sarah," George admitted, his voice thick with emotion. "But none of this would've happened if you hadn't come home."

Sarah smiled. Deep down, she knew the tight-knit Cypressville community would've embraced her grandpa even in her absence. They were a special breed, these folks, bound by genuine care and a fierce sense of community.

The kitchen counters and table groaned under the weight of an epic feast. Jane, a whirlwind of activity, emerged from the kitchen, her arms laden with containers for the overflowing freezer. "Everyone's been bringing casseroles," she explained with a delighted giggle. "Figured you wouldn't have to worry about cooking for a while. I even had to borrow an extra freezer from Mr. Albright – ran out of space!"

Sarah settled her grandpa into his recliner, the warmth of the gathering enveloping them both. One by one, their friends and neighbors ambled over to greet George, their faces etched with relief and joy.

Suddenly, Alex stepped forward, a child's plastic sword clutched in his hand and a regal blue folder tucked under his arm.

"What in tarnation is all this?" George boomed, a hint of suspicion coloring his voice.

Alex cleared his throat, assuming a mock-serious demeanor. "I, Alexander Holstead, of Nova Scotia, do hereby present to you, George Holstead, this title deed to one square foot of land in the sovereign nation of Scotland!" He flourished the folder dramatically.

A wave of laughter rippled through the room as George peered inside, his face breaking into a wide grin. Sarah, her curiosity burning, snatched the folder and skimmed the contents.

"Is this legit?" she exclaimed, her eyes sparkling with amusement.

Alex winked. "Found it online and couldn't resist. Expedited shipping, of course."

Sarah raised the folder in a toast. "Well, Grandpa," she declared, "looks like you're officially a lord... a leaping lord, that is!"

A roar of laughter erupted, and George, his heart brimming with love and gratitude, surveyed the scene before him. He was home, surrounded by loved ones, and the future, like the twinkling Christmas lights that adorned his yard, stretched out before him, full of warmth, promise, and a touch of delightful absurdity.

****

Sarah snuggled deeper into the blanket, the cool night air a stark contrast to the warmth radiating from Alex beside her. The gentle sway of the porch swing mimicked the rhythm of their hearts, still pounding from their passionate kiss just moments ago. Sarah ached to talk about their future, but with Alex's departure looming in just three days, the timing never felt right to talk about it. She wanted to tell him she loved him, but fear stopped her, and a tiny voice whispered hope that he might say it first.

Suddenly, the gentle hum of Alex's phone shattered the peaceful silence. He fished it out of his pocket, a furrow creasing his brow as he glanced at the screen. "It's Benson," he explained. "Do you mind if I take this?"

Sarah forced a smile, masking the knot of worry tightening in her stomach. "Of course, go ahead," she replied, rising to her feet and gathering their empty mugs. "I'll make us some more hot cider."

He leaned in, placing a tender kiss on her cheek. "It won't take long." With that, he pressed the phone to his ear, his voice tinged with excitement as he greeted his friend.

Alone with her thoughts, Sarah busied herself in the kitchen, stealing glances at the clock as the minutes ticked by. Fifteen excruciating minutes later, she ventured back outside, anticipation twisting in her gut. But before she could even touch the screen door, a sharp, angry tone from Alex sent a jolt through her.

His words were like a punch to the gut: "...there is no way in hell I would ever give everything up for a woman."

The air rushed out of her lungs, replaced by a crushing weight that settled in her chest. Tears welled up, blurring her vision. She didn't need to hear more. The picture was clear, a stark reality replacing the fairytale she'd dared to dream.

The harsh reality was a bitter pill to swallow. She was just another "puck bunny" to him, a fleeting fancy and not someone he'd consider building a life with. Shame and a crushing sense of naivety washed over her. How could she have been so foolish?

Tears welled up in her eyes, blurring her vision. Leaving the mugs forgotten on the counter, she fled to the bathroom, seeking refuge. The roar of the faucet and the rush of water masked her sobs as she let out the full force of her heartache. Splashing cold water on her face, she took a shaky breath, reaching for the eyedrops to soothe the telltale signs of her emotional turmoil.

Gazing into the mirror, her reflection held the image of a heartbroken woman, but also a flicker of determination. "I won't let him see my pain," she whispered, her voice trembling. "Two more days, and then I can grieve privately."

Memories of her competitive days surfaced, a mantra echoing in her mind: "You've got this, Sarah. You are strong, capable, and you can win." This time, the victory wasn't about a trophy or a medal, but about maintaining her dignity and protecting her heart. It wasn't ideal, but at least he wouldn't have the satisfaction of witnessing her devastation.

Taking a deep, cleansing breath, Sarah straightened her shoulders. The future remained uncertain, but one thing was clear – she would emerge from this stronger, her heart a little wiser, and her spirit unbroken.

CHAPTER FIFTEEN

THE END OF THE BEGINNING

On the other end of the phone, Benson launched into a familiar diatribe about his latest entanglement, a woman using emotional manipulation tactics to snag a ring. Then turned it all around and started harping on Sarah as if she would be that kind of woman. Alex's frustration crackled through the phone line. "Sarah is nothing like those women, and I can guarantee you," his voice tight with annoyance. "There is no way in hell I would ever give everything up and move for a woman," he declared, then added, "that I didn't respect and love."

"Alright, alright," Benson conceded, a hint of amusement creeping into his voice. "I know, I know. You're not me. Just venting here, you know? This latest girlfriend is trying to guilt me into marriage, and..." He trailed off, shaking his head in exasperation.

"Look, man, I'm sorry you keep getting tangled up in bad relationships," Alex sighed, the anger receding. "But that's not me and Sarah. She's the first woman I've ever dated that..." He hesitated, searching for the right words. "That I would actually consider retiring for."

The silence on the other end was deafening. Without missing a beat, Benson switched the call to video, a bandage adorning a fresh bruise – a souvenir from his latest game. "Are you insane?" Benson sputtered, finally finding his voice.

"No, Jay," Alex countered, a warmth spreading through him at the use of Benson's given name. "Honestly, I've never felt this way before. Twenty-four hours here, and it feels like... home. Even my parents' house doesn't feel this comfortable." He paused, trying to articulate his pull towards this small southern town and its people.

Benson whistled, a low, impressed sound. "Damn, boy. You have it bad. You never call me Jay. Never thought the love bug would actually snag you."

A sheepish grin tugged at Alex's lips. "It did, and bad. There's something special about this community, Sarah, her grandpa... it all feels right, you know?"

Benson took a long pull from his beer, and the wheels seemed to turn in his mind. "Well, then how about this," he declared, a new determination hardening his features. "I fly out tomorrow, meet everyone, and then we can catch a flight back together."

Alex chuckled. "Hold on there, buddy. You'd have to share a room with me at the B&B, and you know I like to hog the covers."

"Yeah, yeah," Benson brushed him off. "Seriously though, Alex, I want to meet these people, especially if they're stealing you away from hockey. Bro code and all that. Gotta make sure they're sane before I let my little brother even consider retiring before our contract's up."

"Whoa, whoa, whoa," Alex held up a hand, defusing the dramatics. "Don't get mushy on me yet, Benson. I didn't say I was retiring. Just that Sarah's the first woman who's ever made me think there might be something more out there than hockey."

Benson whistled again, a long, drawn-out sound. "This is unbelievable. Alright, alright. I'll be there tomorrow. I'll text you when my flight lands."

With that, the call ended. Alex glanced at the clock – later than he thought. He scanned the porch, hoping to see Sarah, but she was nowhere to be seen. He almost wished Sarah had been there to hear the end of his conversation. It would have been the perfect lead-in to a conversation about their future. But with her grandpa's health still a concern, he didn't want to burden her with more worries.

He decided to give her space — time to process everything. Once things settled with George, he could tell her he was falling in love with her, share his hopes and dreams, and see if hers aligned with his. A future together, a life beyond hockey—it all seemed a lot more real now, fueled by a newfound determination and the warmth of Sarah's presence in his life.

Alex entered the house to find Sarah emerging from the bathroom, her face drawn with exhaustion.

"Hey," he said gently, "sorry the call took so long."

Sarah offered a wan smile. "No worries," she replied in a monotone voice, a stark contrast to her usual warmth. "I'm just going to check on Grandpa."

He noticed she studiously avoided eye contact. A knot of unease tightened in his stomach. "Sarah, is everything alright? Did something happen while I was on the phone?"

She nodded, her lower lip trembling slightly. Tears welled up in her eyes, threatening to spill over.

Taking a deep breath, she forced out the words, "Alex, I want you to know that I appreciate everything you've done for me. But tonight… tonight has to be the end."

Alex's heart lurched. "The end? To what? Us?"

She nodded one firm nod.

"Why?" he stammered, confusion clouding his voice.

A tear escaped, tracing a glistening path down her cheek. She swiped it away angrily. "You need to leave," she said, her voice choked with emotion. "Go back to the B&B."

She reached out and pushed him towards the door, her touch surprisingly firm. Alex was utterly bewildered. What had transpired during his phone call? Did George have a sudden change of heart, disapprove of him after all? Whatever the reason, Sarah clearly needed space. Perhaps Jane would shed some light on the situation when he returned to the B&B.

As Sarah closed the door behind him, Alex blurted out, "I'll see you tomorrow. It's the eleventh day, remember? I'm here to see this..." he trailed off, gesturing vaguely, "until the end."

He saw her lips part as if to protest, but before she could speak, he turned and headed for his rental car, his mind racing with unanswered questions. The weight of her unexplained rejection settled heavily on him, casting a shadow over his earlier optimism.

Sarah leaned back on the door and let the tears fall. This was for the best. Only two more days of the game and she would never have to see him again and her heart could start to mend. At least she learned that he would never commit. It was better this way. She wiped her eyes and took a deep breath, "Really it is," she said to the empty room.

Alex pushed a half-eaten breakfast around his plate, the remnants of scrambled eggs a metaphor for his shattered dreams. Sleep had been elusive, his mind replaying the scene with Sarah on a loop, each iteration ending with the same gut-wrenching rejection.

The revelation in his dreams was a harsh slap of reality. He hadn't simply wanted Sarah in his life; he yearned for a future with her. Long-distance dating, a committed partnership – these thoughts had danced in his mind, but marriage? It had never been a conscious consideration.

Six weeks. That's all the time he'd known her. Yet, in those short weeks, the connection they shared felt undeniable, a perfect harmony he hadn't known existed. How could he have been so wrong? So utterly blind to her true feelings?

A creak of the door pulled him from his internal turmoil. Jane bustled in, her usual chipper demeanor replaced by a look of concern. "Whoa, there," she exclaimed, her eyes widening at his disheveled state. "You look like hell. What happened to you?"

Alex recounted the entire evening for Jane, his voice tinged with confusion and a hint of desperation. He finished with, "So, her mood changed only after I was on the phone. Do you think she might have overheard something she took the wrong way?"

Jane, her brow furrowed in concentration. "Hmm, that's certainly a possibility. Let's see..." Her eyes darted around the room as if searching for a missing puzzle piece. "Was the door open when you were talking to Benson?"

"I... I don't think so," Alex admitted, his memory a little hazy from the night's emotional rollercoaster. "Wait, the door was open, but the screen door was closed."

A glimmer of hope flickered in Jane's eyes. "That's all it takes. Now, what exactly did you say to Benson about Sarah?"

Alex recounted the conversation, emphasizing his newfound feelings for Sarah and his hesitation about leaving hockey behind for a future with her. He ended with, "Maybe she thought I was just using her or something?"

Jane chuckled, shaking her head. "Oh Alex, that's the furthest thing from the truth! Here's what probably happened." She leaned forward, her voice conspiratorial. "Sarah probably heard the part about you not wanting to give everything up for a woman, and I can bet you a million bucks she ran away too fast to hear you say she's the first woman you'd consider doing that for. Classic case of misunderstanding!"

Relief washed over Alex, a wave so powerful it nearly knocked him off his chair. "You think so? But she seemed so sure..."

"Sweetheart," Jane said gently, reminding him of Matilda already, "sometimes the strongest emotions cloud our judgment. Especially when eavesdropping on a private conversation with just snippets of information."

A sheepish grin spread across Alex's face. "So, what should I do? How do I fix this?"

Jane's advice offered a lifeline to Alex's sinking hope. "Space," she emphasized, "give her space today. But don't let this opportunity slip away."

Her eyes gleamed with a mischievous glint. "This afternoon, when we head over for the eleventh-day celebration, find a way to get her alone. Be upfront, Alex. Ask her directly about what happened last night. And then," she leaned forward, her voice dropping to a conspiratorial whisper, "tell her how you feel. Tell her everything – about the dreams, how you never considered marriage until her, and how much she means to you in such a short time."

Alex nodded eagerly, a spark rekindled in his eyes. "That's a great plan, Jane. Thanks, I really owe you one."

"Don't worry about that," Jane chuckled, patting his arm reassuringly. "Now, if you'll excuse me, I have a mission of my own – collecting those pipes for Grandpa's project this afternoon."

As Jane bustled out the door, Alex felt a surge of determination. He would get to the bottom of this misunderstanding. He would talk to Sarah, lay his heart bare, and hope that their connection was strong enough to bridge the gap created by a misinterpreted phone call.

CHAPTER SIXTEEN

STOP RUNNING

Alex pulled into the driveway. "Alright, brace yourself," Alex warned, his voice tight with apprehension. "Don't be surprised if Sarah gives me the deep freeze."

Benson snorted. "What happened to soulmates and happily ever after? You were basically spouting love sonnets about her last night, and now she's giving you the silent treatment? Red flag city, bro, I told you."

Alex parked the car, a frustrated sigh escaping his lips. "No, no, she's not a red flag. Jane and I think she might have overheard part of my call with you yesterday."

"Overheard? Like eavesdropping?" Benson raised an eyebrow. "Not a great look, man. You gotta listen to the whole conversation, not just cherry-pick the juicy bits."

"She wasn't eavesdropping, exactly," Alex clarified. "I probably yelled the part about not giving up everything for a woman. Must've sounded bad without the whole thing."

"Yeah, that'd do it," Benson chuckled. "Half a story can be dangerous, especially when emotions are running high. Best get the whole tea before jumping to conclusions, huh?"

Alex nodded grimly. "Exactly. That's why today's mission is getting her alone and explaining everything. Damage control, big time."

"Sounds like a plan. I'll shoot you an assist," Benson said, his playful demeanor fading to concern. "Just remember, Alex, be honest. Lay it all out there – the dreams, the sudden realization about marriage, how much she means to you in such a short time. If I ever find someone like that, I'd want to keep her and never let her go."

Alex took a deep breath, steeling his nerves. "You're right. Thanks, Jay. Here's hoping honesty can fix this mess."

Sarah stirred the pot of soup simmering on the stove, her back stiff and her gaze fixed on the bubbling liquid. The rhythmic clinking of spoons against a bowl the only sound until Jane burst into the kitchen, "Hello, hello, I come bearing gifts." Jane said as she shook the colorful bag in her hand.

"What is that?" Sarah asked, her voice barely above a whisper.

"This, my dear," Jane declared, thrusting the bag towards Sarah with a mischievous grin, "is eleven pipers piping!"

Sarah's stomach lurched. "Eleven... pipers...?" she stammered, a flicker of dread creeping into her voice.

Jane nodded enthusiastically. "Yep! Tonight's party, remember? We're supposed to give all the men pipes and let them have a good time puffing away."

"Oh, no, you don't!" Sarah exclaimed, her voice laced with sudden panic. "Grandpa just had heart surgery! There will be absolutely no smoking – or anything resembling smoking – in this house, ever again!"

Jane chuckled, "Don't worry, sweetie, there's no tobacco.

Originally, I was planning on getting real pipes for the men to just walk around with, but when I went to Mr. McFarlane's farm, his wife was cleaning and practically ripped the bag of real ones out of my hands! See?"

She held out the bag, revealing an assortment of colorful plastic shapes. "Turns out, these are bubble pipes."

Sarah couldn't help but laugh, the tension finally easing from her shoulders. "Thank goodness for Mrs. McFarlane's cleaning spree! And for keeping Grandpa away from temptation."

A beat of silence hung in the air before Jane spoke again, her voice hesitant. "So, I talked to Alex this morning..."

Sarah felt the blood drain from her face, a cold dread settling in her gut. Her carefully constructed facade crumbled. "What did he say? Was he... was he okay?" Her voice barely rose above a whisper.

Jane's brow furrowed. "He was confused, Sarah. Honestly, so am I. What happened?"

Sarah shrugged, her voice laced with a mixture of resignation and lingering affection. "It's just... things are moving too fast. I've never really dated before, and the idea of a long-distance relationship feels overwhelming. You know, I figured I should test the waters a bit, see what's out there. Alex was a great first, don't get me wrong – charming, funny, a good guy all around. But there's a lot to consider. He's older, Canadian..." Her voice trailed off, the unspoken words hanging heavy in the air   different, unfamiliar territory.

Jane winced, sinking onto a nearby stool. "Oh," she mumbled, the weight of her misunderstanding settling in. "Well, this is awkward. Maybe I overstepped my bounds by meddling."

Sarah set down her spoon, her gaze softening. "What did you do?" she asked gently.

"I, um, told Alex he needed to find you and have a conversation today. I thought you were really into him, and maybe I led him on a bit with how much. I'm so sorry, Sarah. I didn't mean to cause any trouble."

Sarah closed her eyes, taking a deep breath to process everything. She scooped the soup into a bowl, her movements measured. "Well," she sighed, a hint of a smile playing on her lips, "at least now I know to avoid being alone with him. As long as I can manage that, there's no real harm done, right? Plus, you were just trying to be a good friend. I didn't share all my feelings with you because, honestly, they just hit me last night. So, thanks for looking out for me."

The entire evening was a carefully orchestrated dance of avoidance for Sarah. Every muscle in her body tensed at the possibility of encountering Alex. His friend, Benson, had arrived early, his easy charm disarming everyone, especially Matilda. Sarah stole a few glances at Alex, only to find him looking in her direction. Her guard faltered each time, and each time, Alex seemed to make a move to approach her.

As the night wound down and goodbyes were exchanged, Sarah felt a surge of relief when her grandpa requested her assistance to his room. It was a welcome buffer between her and Alex.

Inside the room, however, the tranquility shattered. George, his voice firm, launched into a surprising critique.

"Sarah," he began, his tone leaving no room for argument, "I raised you to be a better person than this."

Startled, Sarah stammered, "What did I do?"

"You're completely ignoring that young man who's been pining after you all night. He's obviously smitten, and you're giving him the cold shoulder. What's gotten into you? At least have a conversation with him instead of letting him mope around."

Sarah's carefully constructed facade crumbled. "But I did

talk to him, last night. I told him it was over and practically pushed him out the door."

George, concern etched on his face, settled on the edge of the bed. "Maybe my memory is failing me, but last night, you were practically glowing around Alex. So how did things go from moonstruck to goodbye without giving him a decent explanation?"

Tears welled up in Sarah's eyes. "I love him, Grandpa, but I overheard him on the phone. He said he'd never give up hockey, or something like that, for a woman. Now my mind is all twisted, but Grandpa," she reached out, her voice trembling, "I don't want to be with someone so closed-minded, who wouldn't even consider changing things."

A wry chuckle escaped George's lips. "Sarah, sometimes I forget how young you are."

Sarah bristled. "What's that supposed to mean?"

"Sweetheart," he said, his voice gentle, "one thing I know for sure is a Holstead heart. When we find the one, they just are. And things, well, they have a way of falling into place."

He squeezed her hands. "Alex might not be blood, but he's a Holstead through and through. Just like your grandma and me – love at first sight. The moment Alex met you, he knew too. That's why he rearranged his schedule, all to spend more time with you. It wasn't a coincidence."

His words struck a chord. "He's nearing the end of his career, Sarah. He knows it. Maybe not this season, maybe not the next, but it's coming. And I guarantee you, he'll find a way to make it work. Besides, did you ever stop to consider you only heard a snippet of the conversation? How long was he on the phone?"

Sarah sniffled, wiping her tears. "Maybe fifteen minutes or so."

A knowing look washed over George's face. "See? You might have overreacted a bit, honey. You're inexperienced, that's all. But open communication is key in any relationship, even if it stings. You need to talk to Alex, explain your feelings, how his words hurt you. He's not a bad man, Sarah, but his words bruised your pride. Before you throw away what fate might have intended, shouldn't you give him a chance to explain himself?"

Sarah felt a wave of shame wash over her. Running away, refusing to communicate – it wasn't her, not the way she was raised. Her grandpa was right. She owed Alex an explanation, a chance to bridge the gap created by a misunderstanding.

With newfound determination, she planted a kiss on his cheek. "Thank you, Grandpa. I'm going to see if Alex is still here."

"And if he's not?"

A glint of her Holstead spirit returned to her eyes. "Then I'll text him. We need to talk, tomorrow."

George chuckled. "That's my girl. A fighter till the end."

Sarah smiled, the weight of her decision lifting slightly. "Goodnight, Grandpa."

Relief washed over Sarah, seeing Jane cleaning up the living area. That was until Jane, ever the loyal friend, to her she had cleared the air with Alex, now the damage was done. Alex, assuming their connection was a dead end, had decided to leave town that very night.

Sarah's heart hammered against her ribs. She had to see him, to explain the misunderstanding, the tangled mess of her emotions. The fear of losing him, the love she hadn't dared to admit even to herself – it all came crashing down on her.

"No, Jane," she gasped, clinging to the counter for support. "I lied to you. I love Alex. I did overhear something, but it was all a misunderstanding. Now, because of my lie, I've probably lost him forever."

Tears welled up in her eyes. "He'll never forgive me. He'll

see how immature I am and..." her voice choked off, the rest of the sentence lost in a sob.

Jane, ever resourceful, sprang into action. Grabbing her purse and keys, she dashed towards George's room. "Grandpa George, this is Jane!" she called out, the urgency evident in her voice. "Will you be alright for a couple of hours?"

The door creaked open, revealing George's concerned face. "What's going on, Janie?"

Sarah followed close behind, guilt gnawing at her. "I messed up again," she confessed, her voice barely a whisper.

Jane took over, wasting no time. "I told Alex Sarah was done with him," she blurted out.

"It's not all her fault," Sarah chimed in, her voice choked with emotion. "I lied to her first, Jane."

Jane, wasting no time, continued, "Alex and Benson left tonight. They're on their way to the airport. Benson called his friend who was staying at a hotel near the airport to sleep before leaving. They are supposed to take off in about an hour. Alex figured there was no point in staying."

George, a man of action, didn't hesitate. "Go!" he boomed. "Go get him, Sarah! Take your time, sort things out. Walter can come back and keep me company. But don't you dare come back until you've straightened everything out with Alex, understand?"

A surge of determination replaced the despair in Sarah's eyes. With a grateful kiss on her grandpa's cheek, she turned towards Jane. The race was on. They had to catch Alex before he left town, before the misunderstanding solidified into a permanent goodbye.

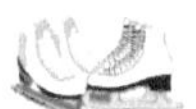

Alex's heart hammered against his ribs as they pulled into the deserted airport. Benson had been an endless fountain of optimism throughout the drive, starkly contrasting Alex's churning emotions. Disappointment had curdled into a dull ache as miles ticked by, leaving him with a heavy sense of what might have been.

Alex and Benson stood outside the deserted airport, the quiet punctuated only by the wail of the approaching storm. Disappointment hung heavy in the air, a physical weight pressing down on Alex's shoulders. Reaching his destination, only to have fate intervene with a thick fog grounding all flights, felt like a cruel twist of the knife.

"Looks like we're stuck here until morning," Benson announced, hanging up his phone. "Pilot's back at his hotel, weather's too bad to fly."

Alex slumped onto a nearby bench, a sigh escaping his lips. "What do we do now? I can't believe we're back here."

"Relax," Benson said with a shrug. "I'll call some hotels and see if they offer airport shuttles. We should've kept the rental car a little longer, huh?"

"Yeah, hindsight's 20/20, huh? Remember that time in Vancouver? Stuck outside the train station, sleeping on the benches?"

The memory brought a chuckle to Benson's lips. "How could I forget? At least it's not raining here."

A small smile tugged at Alex's lips at the memory. The shared experience offered a brief respite from his swirling emotions. Thirty minutes ticked by, Benson's calls proving fruitless. No hotels with shuttles, all car services closed for the night. "Small-town living," Benson muttered, summarizing their predicament.

Silence settled once more, broken only by the howling wind. Alex stared out at the darkness, a knot of unease twisting in his gut. Leaving felt wrong, an inexplicable pull urging him to stay.

As the silence settled between them, Benson broke it first. "Sorry things didn't work out the way you planned, man."

Alex sighed, a heavy weight settling in his chest. "It all feels...off. Deep down, I know Sarah's the one. Her sudden change of heart just doesn't make sense. I wish she'd talked to me instead of shutting me out. But after tonight, it's clear she doesn't want me around."

His words hung in the air, heavy with resignation. Suddenly, a screech of tires shattered the quiet, a car careening around the bend into the airport driveway at breakneck speed.

"What the hell?" Benson exclaimed, his voice laced with alarm.

Alex squinted through the darkness. "That's Jane's car! What's she doing here?"

The answer arrived when the car barely screeched to a stop and in a flash of movement. Sarah, tears streaming down her face, leaped out of the passenger seat and practically launched herself at Alex. Her arms wrapped around his neck, legs clinging to his waist, her sobs muffled against his chest.

Alex, stunned into speechlessness, held her close, his heart pounding a frantic rhythm against his ribs. "Sarah? What's going on?"

Sarah clung to him, refusing to let go. "I'm so stupid, Alex! I was scared. Please, please don't leave!"

The raw emotion in her voice washed over him, dissolving his confusion. He held her tighter, whispering reassurances into her hair. "Hey, hey, what's all this about?"

Taking a deep, shuddering breath, Sarah pulled back slightly, her eyes glistening with tears. "I love you," she confessed, her voice trembling. "My pride might be bruised, but I couldn't let you leave thinking I didn't care. I know you never want to move here, and that's okay. You don't have to give up hockey. But even if this is goodbye, I needed you to know."

Her eyes locked with his, a desperate plea shimmering in their depths. "If there's even a shred of a chance you feel the same way," she continued, her voice dropping to a whisper, "I would love to try long distance. And maybe..." she took another shaky breath, "...maybe you could stay until the end of the twelfth day of Christmas like planned?"

Alex didn't say a word; he kissed her and kissed her again. Benson whistled, and Jane was laughing, crying, and clapping. But Alex tuned them out and solely focused on Sarah. "I love you too, and you didn't hear the whole conversation. I would never move for a woman I didn't love or trust, and you, Sarah, are worthy of both."

EPILOGUE

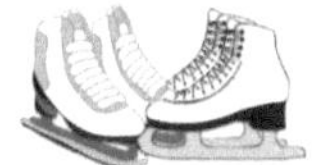

The town hall bustled with activity as the council members gathered for their Christmas planning meeting. Mayor Albright, ever the advocate for change, had proposed a fresh approach to the annual festival. Discussions swirled around boosting tourism, and Jane, Sarah, and Alex found themselves reminiscing about their "Twelve Days of Christmas" adventure nearly six years ago, amidst the brainstorming session.

Andrea, her gaze softening, turned to her husband, Frank. "That's where it all began for us, wasn't it?" she murmured, a trace of nostalgia in her voice. Frank squeezed her hand, his eyes reflecting the same sentiment. "Indeed," he replied, leaning in to plant a kiss on her knuckles. "And I'm eternally grateful for that serendipitous twist of fate."

Sarah, visibly pregnant, shifted in her seat. A gentle smile played on her lips. "Grandpa would be beaming down on us from above if we did it again," she mused. "He absolutely adored the whole thing, and look at us all now," she swept her gaze around the table, her eyes twinkling, "because of that event, Alex and I own an ice rink and are still in

Cypressville with a new generation on the way! Grandpa must be jumping for joy over all of us being together."

Andrea, wielding a small gavel, brought the room to order. "Well, that settles it then," she declared. "We're reviving the Twelve Days of Christmas! Let's bring Blair back to handle the broadcasting. She can interview the past participants and gather some interesting content."

Megan, Susan's daughter, who had been engrossed in a book, perked up at the news. "This could be even more exciting if we turn it into a town-wide scavenger hunt!" she exclaimed. "Imagine if everyone had to create and find things that fit the song and the best and most creative one won a grand prize!"

Melissa, ever the enthusiastic supporter, chimed in, "Megan, that's absolutely brilliant!"

Megan beamed, muttering a grateful "Thanks, Aunt Lissy" before diving back into her book.

Jane, brimming with the spirit of hospitality, couldn't resist adding to the festive plans. "The winner can enjoy a complimentary night's stay at my B&B!" she announced.

Jenna and Max were whispering, and then Max jumped in with another exciting offer: " A new designer gown or suit from our Love by Design trunk show can be another prize!"

Walter chuckled. "Well, I can't be outdone now, can I? How about this: the winner will also receive unlimited free coffee and a delicious gumbo dinner at Main Street Java in memory of George and his love of my contribution of the three French hens that wonderful Christmas."

A wave of laughter rippled through the room.

"All of you, thank you for your generosity," Mayor Albright responded with a warm smile. Susan, would you mind contacting Blair to see if she'd be interested in broadcasting and being a judge? Perhaps Alex, you could convince Jay to join the panel as well? It's been a while since we've seen him. Hopefully, we can find another celebrity to help out and generate some buzz."

Alex chuckled. "Hey now, I'm not that forgotten, am I?"

Andrea, the epitome of fairness, shook her head. "You know very well council members can't judge. That wouldn't be right."

"I know, I know, just teasing," Alex conceded. "But in any case, I'll definitely talk to Jay. Since his retirement, I'm sure he'd be happy to participate."

The room buzzed with excitement as the planning session unfolded. The "Twelve Days of Christmas" was back, bigger and better than ever, promising a season of joy, connection, and a whole lot of fun for the entire town. And it all began with a simple act of honesty, a dash of serendipity, and the courage to chase after love.

WALTER'S LOUISIANA GUMBO

Nestled in the heart of Cypressville, Main Street Java isn't just a coffee shop, it's a haven built with love by Walter. After years dedicated to another career, Walter returned home in 2001 with a dream – to breathe life back into his beloved community. The old warehouse and department store became a canvas, and Walter, the artist, transformed it into a vibrant space for laughter, conversation, and most importantly, connection. It's a place where teenagers find a safe haven, families gather over steaming cups of joe, and during those crisp winter months, the aroma of Walter's legendary gumbo draws everyone "out of the woodwork," warming bellies and hearts alike. This recipe isn't just a collection of ingredients, it's a taste of Walter's family history. This recipe is his mother Johnnie Bernadette's, and it's a cooking tradition passed down with the love of bringing folks together. Main Street Java itself is a reflection of that love for Cypressville, and an invitation to join the warmth that simmers within its walls. So, grab your favorite mug, turn the page, and let Walter's gumbo, a taste of family and community, bring a little bit of Cypressville magic into your kitchen.

INGREDIENTS

- Roux
- 2 quarts chicken stock (Walter uses Swanson® 100% Natural Gluten Free Chicken Cooking Stock)
- 2 quarts water
- 1 large yellow onion
- Okra
- Garlic powder
- Red pepper flakes
- Cajun Seasoning (Walter uses Tony Chachere's® Original Creole Seasoning)
- Black pepper
- Salt
- 2 large boneless, skinless chicken breast or 6 boneless, skinless chicken thighs
- 3 links of sausage (Walter prefers Andouille Sausage)

GETTING STARTED

First, you will need to know how to make a roux. The color of the roux is very important to a good base for your gumbo. Walter likes it colored between Chicken/Sausage Gumbo and Seafood Gumbo for his recipe.

HOW TO MAKE A ROUX

- **Homemade Roux**- Equal parts oil and flour in a cast iron or stainless pan (do not use nonstick!) on medium-high heat. Generally 1 tablespoon flour/1 tablespoon fat roux per cup of liquid.
- 4 tbsp flour/ 4 tbsp Vegetable Oil
- Whisk the flour into the oil. Stir continuously until you have a smooth, thick paste that is a rich, almost chocolate brown - but not burnt. If it's too thick to whisk, add a little more oil. If it seems runny, add more flour.
- Add sliced Andouille sausage at the end to brown the sausage and keep the roux from burning. If not

using sausage, chicken or vegetables (okra) can be used at the end, but do not use shrimp; it will cause them to overcook and be tough.

- **Short cut roux**- For those who prefer a quicker method, fear not. 4 heaping tablespoons of dark roux (SAVOIE'S® Old Fashioned Dark Roux) to 4 quarts liquid is all you need. Bring it to a boil for ½ hour, and you'll still achieve a flavorful gumbo.

COOKING INSTRUCTIONS

STEP ONE

- Preheat oven to 350
- Season the chicken with salt, pepper, and garlic powder
- Bake for about 40 minutes

STEP TWO HOMEMADE ROUX MIX

- Make a dark roux following instructions on how to make a roux. (It should be dark brown but not burnt. See kristentassin.com/gumbo to see a roux chart with the proper color)

STEP THREE HOMEMADE ROUX MIX

- To the homemade roux mix add okra and sliced

Andouille sausage at the end to brown the sausage and keep the roux from burning.
- Scrape the roux and sausage mixture into a large stock pot (beware of the spatter).

IN THE LARGE STOCK POT

- Roux Mix
- 2 quarts of chicken stock
- 2 quarts of water
- Diced onions
- Add seasoning
- Add cooked chicken
- Bring to a boil
- Let simmer for an hour to three hours to absorb the flavors
- Stir occasionally

STEP TWO ROUX IN A JAR

- 4 heaping tablespoons of dark roux (SAVOIE'S® Old Fashioned Dark Roux)
- 2 quarts of chicken stock
- 2 quarts of water
- Bring it to a boil for ½ hour, and you'll still achieve a flavorful gumbo.
- Add Diced onions
- Add seasoning (salt, pepper, red pepper flakes, cajun seasoning to taste)
- Add cooked chicken
- Bring to a boil
- Let simmer for an hour to three hours to absorb flavors.

- Stir occasionally.

Served like a soup, with a scoop of white rice. Here in Central Louisiana, we like to have country potato salad as a side. The potato salad tastes amazing when a spoonful at a time is dipped into the gumbo.

Enjoy!

LAGNIAPPE

COUNTRY POTATO SALAD

POTATO SALAD INGREDIENTS

- 6 Idaho potatoes
- 6 boiled eggs
- Helmann's® Mayonnaise (Walter uses only this brand; he believes nothing else tastes better.)
- Salt
- Pepper
- Cap of Distilled Vinegar

COOKING INSTRUCTIONS

- Shave the potatoes and boil in salted water
- Hard boil the eggs
- In a large bowl mash the potatoes
- Cut the eggs separate yolks and whites
- Chop the whites into small pieces
- In a separate bowl mix all the cooked egg yolks with mayonnaise salt pepper and vinegar

- Combine the mixture and ¾ of the chopped whites into the mashed potatoes and mix well
- Add more mayonnaise to create a smooth consistency
- Add more salt and pepper to taste
- The potato salad should be smooth with some chunks

Serve warm as a side dish to Gumbo.

A MOMENT OF YOUR TIME

Enjoyed this book? Please leave a review!

Reviews help indie authors like me reach new readers and help new readers decide if a book is for them.

Please take a moment to write a short review.

Thank you! Your support means the world to me, and I'm truly grateful for your time and feedback. Click HERE or scan the QR code to leave a sentence or two.

BOOK EXTRAS!

Visit my website, where you can find extra goodies, such as images of the city, the cast, and merchandise for all my books and series.

https://kristentassin.com/cypressville

To stay in touch and be the first to find out about big news, book series, and giveaways, sign up for my newsletter at www.kristentassin.com. As an incentive, you will receive my first book ever written, a FREE Christmas in Cypressville ebook.

ACKNOWLEDGMENTS

To Tina, my writing partner, thank you for the countless cups of coffee, the pep talks that got me over writer's block, and for always believing this story could find its way into the world. Your unwavering support means everything to me.

To my sister Bernie, if you hadn't introduced me to the quirky world of Stars Hollow in Gilmore Girls, I don't think Cypressville would have ever been born. Thanks for sparking the love of a close-knit community!

To my Mastermind group - Kat, Jenn, Holly, and Sarah - your insights and camaraderie have been invaluable. Thank you for sharing your publishing knowledge and for being a constant source of encouragement. You all are true gems!

To Elizabeth, my best friend and chosen sister, thank you for being my partner in imagination since childhood. Your creativity has always pushed me to dream bigger.

To everyone who has patiently listened to me ramble on about my book and characters, you're the absolute best. Your unwavering support fueled my passion for this story.

And lastly, but most significantly, to my two beautiful daughters who have not just believed in my dreams, but have been the very inspiration behind them. Your love, loyalty, and unwavering support are not just cherished, they are the heartbeat of this book. This book is not just for you, it is because of you.

ABOUT THE AUTHOR

Kristen Tassin is an independent author whose lifelong passion for storytelling ignited into a full-fledged career. Overcoming the challenges of dysgraphia, she dedicated years to honing her craft while balancing motherhood and a demanding career. A hopeless romantic at heart, Kristen has always believed in the power of happily ever afters. Her southern roots and love for cozy winter vibes provide the perfect backdrop for her writing.

With a diverse background as a single mother, cosmetologist, and mental health advocate, Kristen infuses her stories with authenticity and depth. Her experiences interacting with people from all walks of life have shaped her ability to create compelling characters and captivating worlds.

Kristen's writing explores a range of genres, from the heartwarming charm of small-town romances to the enchanting realms of fantasy. Her dedication to mental health representation shines through in her work, offering readers relatable and empowering narratives.

Keep in touch, sign up for my newsletter at www.kristentassin.com

facebook.com/author.kristentassin

instagram.com/kristentassin.author

tiktok.com/@kristentassin.author

amazon.com/stores/Kristen-Tassin/author/B0982VMXZ

ALSO BY KRISTEN TASSIN

CONTEMPORARY ROMANCE

Cypressville Small Town Romance

Christmas in Cypressville

Love by Design

Love Under Construction

Christmas on Ice

FANTASY ROMANCE | SHORT READS

Neotropolis Bites

Fatal Grace

Small Town Short Reads: Alien Romance

Unexpected Destiny (Anthology)

Small Town Short Reads: Paranormal Matchmaker Romance

The Ghost in Apartment 99B

Tapestry of Fated Dreams

Land of Nod (Fairytales)

Woven in Dreams

www.ingramcontent.com/pod-product-compliance
Lightning Source LLC
Chambersburg PA
CBHW021000160726
47994CB00006B/2312